Her mo_____tay
a_____

Men whose eyes could undress you and possess you in the self-same glance. Men whose toughness in word and manner covered their feelings. Men whose rough hands conjured up unladylike images of silken bodies entwined. Men who could break your heart just as surely as they could break a wild mustang and abandon you the instant you were tamed....

But despite her mother's warning, Carrie felt herself unable to resist the enigmatic cowboy.

Dear Reader,

What a special lineup of love stories Silhouette Romance has for you this month. Bestselling author Sandra Steffen continues her BACHELOR GULCH miniseries with *Clayton's Made-Over Mrs.* And in *The Lawman's Legacy*, favorite author Phyllis Halldorson introduces a special promotion called MEN! Who says good men are hard to find?! Plus, we've got Julianna Morris's *Daddy Woke up Married*—our BUNDLES OF JOY selection—*Love, Marriage and Family 101* by Anne Peters, *The Scandalous Return of Jake Walker* by Myrna Mackenzie and *The Cowboy Who Broke the Mold* by Cathleen Galitz, who makes her Silhouette debut as one of our WOMEN TO WATCH.

I hope you enjoy all six of these wonderful novels. In fact, I'd love to get your thoughts on Silhouette Romance. If you'd like to share your comments about the Silhouette Romance line, please send a letter directly to my attention: Melissa Senate, Senior Editor, Silhouette Books, 300 E. 42nd St., 6th Floor, New York, NY 10017. I welcome all of your comments, and here are a few particulars I'd like to have your feedback on:

1) Why do you enjoy Silhouette Romance?
2) What types of stories would you like to see more of? Less of?
3) Do you have favorite authors?

Your thoughts about Romance are very important to me. After all, these books are for you! Again, I hope you enjoy our six novels this month—and that you'll write me with your thoughts.

Regards,

Melissa Senate
Senior Editor
Silhouette Books

Please address questions and book requests to:
Silhouette Reader Service
U.S.: 3010 Walden Ave., P.O. Box 1325, Buffalo, NY 14269
Canadian: P.O. Box 609, Fort Erie, Ont. L2A 5X3

THE COWBOY WHO BROKE THE MOLD

Cathleen Galitz

R O M A N C E™

Published by Silhouette Books

America's Publisher of Contemporary Romance

To Brian—the man who,
in a world beleaguered by bottom-liners,
puts us first.

 SILHOUETTE BOOKS

ISBN 0-373-19257-6

THE COWBOY WHO BROKE THE MOLD

This edition published by arrangement with Harlequin Books S.A.

® and TM are trademarks of Harlequin Books S.A., used under license.
Trademarks indicated with ® are registered in the United States Patent
and Trademark Office, the Canadian Trade Marks Office and in other
countries.

Printed in U.S.A.

CATHLEEN GALITZ,

a Wyoming native, teaches English to students in grades seven to twelve in a rural school that houses kindergartners and seniors in the same building. She lives in a small Wyoming town with her husband and two children. When she's not busy writing, teaching or working with her Cub Scout den, she can most often be found hiking or snowmobiling in the Wind River Mountains.

The Silhouette Spotlight
"Where Passion Lives"

™

MEET WOMAN TO WATCH *Cathleen Galitz*

What was your inspiration for
THE COWBOY WHO BROKE THE MOLD?

CG: "For one of our wedding anniversaries, my husband booked us a romantic getaway at historic Miner's Delight in Atlantic City. We danced the night away in a saloon where a fun-loving group of cowboys drowned out ghostly whispers from the past. A jackalope winking at me above our table set my mind whirling faster than the couples on the dance floor. From this unique setting, the seed for my book was planted."

What about the Romance line appeals
to you as a reader and as a writer?

CG: "Many of my favorite authors are in this line, and I am thrilled to join them in writing the kind of books that I myself love to read—heartwarming, genuine stories that are driven by tender romance rather than sex alone."

Why is this book special to you?

CG: "This is my first published novel. I think the humor and the characters themselves make the book stand out. Carrie and Judson stepped right off the page and into my heart. I sometimes have trouble remembering that they aren't real!"

Chapter One

Judson Horn had no more difficulty in picking out the new schoolteacher as she stepped off the plane at Rock Springs than if she had been holding a gigantic placard. Ms. Carrie Raben was, after all, exactly what he had expected.

The dark-haired cowboy shook his head in disgust. "No more sense than a calf straying into a barbecue," he muttered to himself.

Wearing a matching dark skirt and blazer, and sporting an expensive leather briefcase, Ms. Raben looked infinitely better suited to running an executive board meeting than to teaching a raggle-taggle group of schoolchildren in the middle of nowhere. Her light brown hair was cut in a chin-length bob that swung neatly with her every movement. It was precisely the no-nonsense sort of hairdo Judson had the woman figured for before he'd ever laid eyes on her.

It took less than a minute for Judson Horn to size Ms. Raben up as just another lost cause from back East.

He'd had his bellyful of 'em—those cosmopolitan types who insisted on accompanying their husbands deep into the backwoods on the hunting expeditions he guided. Without fail they were whining, spoiled creatures who wanted to go home the day after he had set up camp. To them he was merely an anomaly of nature—a blue-eyed half-breed who piqued their cultural curiosity. Despite their obsequious panderings to the plight of the American Indian, what most of these social matrons really wanted was a savage lover to turn their blue blood to fire.

Stoically detached in the face of their not-so-subtle advances, Judson merely had to run a finger across the scar tissue along his jaw to remember an encounter with a couple of overly protective brothers who took a strong personal dislike to his relationship with their lily-white sister....

"You half-breed bastard!" they had called out as the lash of the whip sailed through the air, cut into the tender flesh across his back and curled around his jaw. *"People 'round here don't take to Indian trash messing with their women."*

Judson swallowed hard against the rage that rose in his chest at the memory and made himself focus on the task at hand—transporting a hothouse orchid to the harsh clime of Wyoming. He gave the pretty little thing less than a month before she came to the realization that she was totally unsuited for the rigors of living in the wild Wild West.

I've signed a contract to teach in hell, Carrie thought to herself, ducking to avoid hitting her head on the exit ramp door. Greeted by a blast of hot wind, she clutched the wobbly railing and took her first step in Wyoming.

Long before the eighteen-passenger airplane touched down in the middle of what appeared to be a gigantic dust bowl, it had managed to hit every air pocket in the state with an astonishing accuracy that left Carrie feeling sick to her stomach. From an altitude of twenty-five thousand feet, it appeared that the entire state was devoid of human life—a world of vast nothingness where colors all blurred to varying shades of brown. And now viewing her new home at eye level, Carrie had to admit that it was, indeed, as bleak as it had appeared from so high above. Truly this was the epitome of nowhere.

Where were all the mountains her favorite authors had so eloquently eulogized in their novels? she wondered. Where was the sense of freedom she had anticipated feeling with the first rush of fresh air into her citified lungs? And where, for that matter, was Bill Madden with his promised open-armed Western hospitality?

Fighting the wind, Carrie made her way to the airport terminal. She looked around the tiny lobby in dismay, her green eyes searching the area, trying to match a face to the slightly desperate voice that had hired her sight unseen over the telephone. In her mind, she pictured an overweight, balding man wearing a suit the color of a pastel mint.

"Mommy!" squealed the precocious six-year-old whose incessant chatter had inundated the tiny aircraft for the past two and a half hours. "Mommy," he repeated louder, tugging at her sleeve and pointing. "Look, a real-live cowboy! I thought they were dead...like the dinosaurs—"

"Terry!" whispered his harried-looking mother through clenched teeth. "How many times do I have to tell you it's not polite to point?"

Following the direction of Terry's extended index finger, Carrie found herself looking up into the sexiest sky-blue eyes she'd ever encountered. Her stomach lurched to her throat as if she had just hit another air pocket. Standing not two feet away was a broad-shouldered man who looked like he'd just walked off a Western movie set. She indulged herself in a long look, one that started with a black felt Stetson hat, lingered over a silver belt buckle and ended with a pair of snakeskin cowboy boots.

"Mr. M-Madden?" she stammered.

A slow smile spread across the man's rugged features. "No, ma'am. Bill couldn't make it so he asked me to pick you up and pack you to Harmony."

Carrie's temperature soared. Taking a deep breath of air, she tried to combat the sense of light-headedness that she wanted to believe was simply the aftereffect of a jarring plane ride. Never before had she seen such electric blue eyes on such a dark-complexioned man. The effect was so startling it left her positively breathless.

Grabbing four heavy bags marked with her tags from the luggage carousel, he balanced two of them under his long arms much the way Carrie imagined one would lug bales of hay to a starving herd of cattle and started toward the doorway without another word. Picking up her lighter bags, she mutely followed the lanky cowboy out of the airport and into the bright August sunshine. The way those tight Wrangler jeans hugged his narrow hips as he swaggered across the parking lot was absolutely hypnotic. Her eyes would not release their hold on the rhythmic swaying of his jeans. So absorbed was she in the view that when he stopped abruptly in front of her, Carrie bumped right into him.

"Excuse me," she mumbled, red-faced.

Though he merely nodded in reply, the man's crooked grin left Carrie with the disquieting sense that he knew exactly what she was thinking. As she watched her "chauffeur" dump all of her bags into the back of a dilapidated pickup that had seen better days, she wondered whether her first task at Harmony would be to clean the manure off the expensive luggage her parents had given her as a going away present.

Wiping his hands on his jeans, the man stepped back and opened the passenger side door for her.

Eager to prove capable of fending for herself in the Equality State, Carrie announced with a determined smile, "Thank you, but I can do that for myself."

"Yes, ma'am," the cowboy said, tilting back his hat. Seemingly looking right through her, that damnable grin affixed on his face, he stepped back and made his way around to the other side of the vehicle. Carrie could swear the air fairly vibrated with the unspoken animosity behind those amazing cerulean eyes.

Climbing into the cab of the pickup, she grappled both with her narrow skirt and the realization that she had somehow inadvertently offended the man's Western sense of gallantry. Feeling his gaze traverse the length of her legs, Carrie primly smoothed out the skirt that had climbed high upon her thighs. Were all Wyoming men so utterly brazen? she wondered, feeling a blush stain her cheeks. That her look of practiced feminine indignation was received with a twinkle of amusement only served to emphasize the feeling that this man was secretly laughing at her.

As the vehicle lurched to life and they headed down the road, Carrie got her first up-close look at Rock Springs, Wyoming. It was as dreary and no-frills as the olive green pickup in which she rode. Set in the middle of a sagebrush-covered desert, the town could best be described as dusty.

"This is pretty much the cultural metropolis of this part of the state," her driver matter-of-factly informed her.

Though a variety of small shops lined the streets, Carrie was immediately struck by the fact that the predominant business in town was essentially escapist. An impressive number of bars and saloons called not only to the fantasies of the tourists but to the plight of Rock Springs's locals, as well. A police car, its lights flashing, was parked outside a tavern named Buster's. A worn-looking blonde in a leather miniskirt slumped on a street corner bench. A drunk struggled against a red light as Carrie watched him make his way from one bar into an equally dismal one across the street. A huge tumbleweed drifted along the sidewalk in a lonesome gust of wind.

As he pointed to the town's infamous red-light district, it occurred to Carrie that her driver had purposely gone out of his way to show her the seedy side of town. Wryly she considered telling him that he was wasting his time if he was trying to shock her. In fact, some of the things she had seen back in Chicago might just set this rough-and-tumble cowboy's charming smile awry.

What actually did shock her was the modern high school they passed on their way out of town. Complete with a well-groomed football field, track and swimming pool, it was far superior to the facilities where she had previously taught.

"Don't get your hopes up. Harmony ain't this nice," the man warned.

"Isn't," she automatically corrected.

Whether it was anger or mirth that activated the dimples at both corners of his mouth, Carrie wasn't sure. Nonetheless, she quickly changed the subject. "Since we're going to be traveling the next one hundred and twenty miles together, it would be nice to know your name."

"Judson Horn at your service, ma'am," he replied, pushing his hat back on his head. "And I can't say as I'd blame you for wanting to teach here instead of in the middle of nowhere."

He flashed her a smile and Carrie felt a peculiar sharp stab deep inside her. The man was entirely too sure of himself, she thought with irritation, noting that even the way he draped one arm over the steering wheel was unnervingly sexy. Judson Horn exuded an aura of self-confidence that might just border on the edge of arrogance. Carrie mentally reviewed her etched-in-stone list of Pitfalls To Avoid In Future. And Arrogant Men was right there at the top.

"I'm sure I'll manage, thank you very much, Mr. Horn," she replied stiffly.

"It's not much of a place for a woman alone, you know. And call me Jud. Unlike the big city, we don't stand on formality around here."

Bristling, Carrie wondered whether the only place this Western Neanderthal thought women belonged was the bedroom and the kitchen—in that order.

Judson Horn's smirk did not diminish in the least at her obvious antipathy. If anything, he seemed to take malevolent pleasure from her disapproval. Sidling closer to the door, Carrie turned her head sharply away and looked out the window, determined to tune out the decidedly handsome stranger with whom she had no choice but to share the next hundred or so miles.

* * *

Jud passed off the new schoolteacher's cold shoulder as typical urbane snobbery. As a rule, outsiders generally considered themselves culturally superior to locals. A man of the land himself, he was certain that only twisted thinking could suppose concrete and skyscrapers preferable to a life in wide-open spaces. His ancestors had been wise in their desire to protect Mother Earth from the white man's butchery, their children from his poisoned thoughts.

It amused him to think that Little Miss Eastern Know-It-All was sorely mistaken in her assumption that he was some two-bit hired hand whom she could dismiss however rudely she pleased. Though he briefly considered clarifying his identity, his rather bent sense of humor stopped him from doing so. It would simply be too much fun to see how sophisticated Ms. Raben would react when she discovered that a half-breed Indian was her new boss!

True, he had fallen into the position by default. And gauging by the volume of public dismay when his appointment to the Board of Trustees had been announced, it would have been wise for him to have simply declined the "honor." Instead, ignoring the raised eyebrows of his neighbors, he'd dug in his heels, determined to prove the patrons of School District No. 4 wrong about him once again.

As if it wasn't enough just raising twin cyclone kids by himself and trying to keep his ranch profitable in tight times, he could do without the headaches that inevitably went along with local politics—particularly for someone of his temperament and dubious background.

But Judson Horn wasn't a man who took the easy way out of anything. Besides, if there was ever a way to protect his own children from the biases that had plagued his own schooling, serving on the school board was the surest way to guarantee the education to which they were entitled. If that meant the twins had to endure some cruel teasing by their classmates, then so be it. He'd endured it. And when all was said and done, he would have to say he was a stronger person because of it.

Even if his biological father had undoubtedly played on the sympathy garnered by his terminal illness to publicly acknowledge the son he'd refused to claim at birth, there wasn't a damned thing Judson could do about his father's deathbed wish. He only knew it must have taken an Academy-Award-winning performance to convince Harmony's strictly anglo Board of Education to accept a bastard half-breed in their hallowed ranks.

Judson fought the anger that rose like bile in his throat. He would have liked the opportunity to tell that sorry excuse for a man not to bother. Coming at the end of a lifetime of denial and betrayal, such a grandiose public gesture had been vulgar at best. At worst, the final joke of a hypocrite who hadn't bothered to claim his illegitimate son when it would have mattered to him. Arthur Christianson had only deluded himself during his last days with the thought that he could somehow buy righteousness and lay claim to his only grandchildren through a last will and testament. It mattered little to Judson that his inheritance was substantial. As far as he was concerned, his old man would spend eternity in hell waiting for his forgiveness.

Eternity and then some.

"What was that?" Carrie asked, interrupting the dark thoughts that cast a shadow across Judson's handsome features.

Her eyes were like those of a child as they followed the movement of a graceful brown and white creature that darted across the road in front of them and slipped beneath the barbed-wire fence lining the highway.

"Haven't you ever seen an antelope before?" he scoffed.

Aware that Judson Horn seemed to think such lack of knowledge was grounds to revoke her teaching certificate, Carrie reluctantly admitted her ignorance.

"Well, you'd better get used to 'em. There are more of those crazy goats than people in this state."

"They're beautiful," she said simply.

"They're a damned nuisance."

Carrie's eyes darted to the gun rack directly behind her head. Speculating on what fate awaited "nuisances" in the State of Wyoming, she clamped her mouth shut.

Judson lifted the hat from his head to wipe the sweat from his brow. The pickup was without air-conditioning, and it was hot, miserably so. Both windows were rolled down, allowing dust to coat everything inside the cab with a dirty film. He had a lot of things to do today, and picking up this silly little greenhorn did little to improve his mood. Though he was tempted to voice a caustic comment about her obvious unsuitability for the job that lay ahead, there was something so utterly wide-eyed about Carrie's excitement that he stayed his tongue. She reminded him of a miller furiously beating its wings against the draw of a light bulb, trying its damnedest to immolate itself.

And she somehow made the experience seem enviable.

Most assuredly there would be time enough for Ms. Raben to realize the mistake she had made. Until then,

Judson decided that there should be no reason why they couldn't coexist amicably. Turning off the interstate and onto a less traveled road, he reached into the small cooler on the seat between them.

"Want something to drink?" he asked, pulling out a cold one.

Carrie cringed.

Drinking and driving made her nervous. Though there wasn't another soul on the road and the likelihood of an accident seemed minimal, her hand tightened on the door handle. It was one thing to be traveling alone with a stranger and quite another to be riding with a drunk.

"No," she stated coolly.

"You sure?" Judson asked with a peculiar look in his eye. He held the cold can to his forehead for a second before pulling the tab and taking a long, cool swig.

Carrie's throat was parched. Inviting beads of moisture dripped down the sides of the can. She had to resist the temptation to dab away the rivulets of sweat forming between her breasts.

"Positive."

A hard glint turned eyes the color of a cloudless sky to gunmetal as he asked, "Even if it's nonalcoholic?"

Again Carrie cringed, this time not out of fear but embarrassment. Without so much as bothering to check the label, she had simply assumed that drinking and driving was de rigueur for the Western male.

"I didn't mean to—"

"Just because I'm an Indian—" Judson's voice was cold enough to drop the temperature in the cab several degrees "— doesn't mean I'm a drunk." He tilted his head back and took an especially long pull.

His words came as a total surprise. An Indian with blue eyes? Carrie was as taken aback both by Judson's declaration of his ancestry as by the vehemence with which it was uttered.

"I didn't think that—"

"I've yet to meet a white who hasn't jumped to the same conclusion as you—that we're all good-for-nothing drunks living off government handouts. You don't need to worry, *Ms. Raben.*" Her name came out as a hiss. "You'll fit in just fine around here."

Carrie drew back as if his words were fists. She had never meant to imply such a thing.

Unmindful of the bewildered look on that pretty face, Judson continued. "There's a long line of alcoholism in my family history, and I can assure you that I've learned something by burying the dead, so you can just let go of that door handle and relax. I have no intention of killing you today."

Tension wrapped the pair in a tight shroud. Gritty and on edge, Carrie attributed her raw nerves to the long, uncomfortable plane ride from Chicago. She refused to give credence to the possibility that her growing sense of uneasiness was linked to an unlikely chauffeur whose earthy scent of woods and sheer masculinity invaded her senses and left her feeling helpless.

"Hell," he grumbled. "If you're afraid of *me,* how are you ever going to cope with the demands of a school smack-dab in the middle of the wilderness?"

"I am not afraid!" Carrie rejoined a little too quickly, a little too loudly. "And—" Her voice rose a notch. "I certainly didn't mean to hurt your feelings!"

Issued with such fierce indignation, it was an odd apology indeed. Judson's eyes snapped from the road to lock upon her. Like an insect squirming beneath a microscope, Carrie was minutely scrutinized.

Judson stared directly into the depths of his passenger's eyes, the color of which, he decided, was the green of aspen leaves, of undiscovered passion and of a raw vulnerability that reached deep down inside him and squeezed his heart—hard. It just didn't make sense. The woman was a living, breathing oxymoron. How could such a frightened, little thing exude sexuality like a teapot giving off steam?

"Don't worry. I'm past having my *feelings* hurt," he muttered in disgust.

It was a bald-faced lie. It bothered him a whole lot more than he liked to admit that his children's pretty new schoolteacher had been so eager to assume the worst about him. By now he should be numb to such umbrage, but the dull ache throbbing in his chest assured him otherwise. Bitterly, Judson congratulated himself for casting the only vote against hiring this woman whose angelic face presented a deceptive facade for the bigotry that had marked his life. He saw it as his duty to protect the children of Harmony from people like Carrie Raben.

Her assumption that he was a drinker couldn't have been further from the truth. As a child he had watched alcohol rob his mother of her youth and beauty, slowly destroying her. Through the eyes of an adult, he witnessed the desiccation of an entire culture. By publicly taking the pledge that bound him to a life of sobriety, he hoped to provide the kind of positive role model that young Native American men and women so desperately needed. Judson vowed his own children would never grow up in a home like the one in which he was raised—one in which a bottle held greater priority than food on the table or paid utilities.

Defiantly, he reminded himself that just because Carrie Raben's singular looks seemed to grow on him with each passing mile, that didn't make her any better than anyone else who passed judgment on him without bothering to look past the color of his skin.

Carrie was burning up. The open windows let in fresh air but did little to lower the temperature in the cab. Staring at a sky that met the horizon in an unbroken, infinite line, she was struck by the sheer enormity of the open range that was as intimidating as the virile man sitting a mere arm's length away. It was apparent that she and her driver were as different as night and day, as explosive as gasoline and matches...

As the old green pickup rolled off the main road and rumbled onto a dirt one, Judson unsnapped the top two buttons of his Western shirt and opened his chest to the air rushing in the open window. Carrie was getting hotter by the minute, and not because of the desert heat. Surely the man knew he was giving off sexual vibes that could ignite a prairie fire. Her own fingers itched to untie the silk bow wilting around her neck. An unexpected thought flitted across her mind, an X-rated image of Judson Horn pulling off to the side of the road and slowly undressing her— Carrie dropped the thought like a burning match. She hardly knew him and here she was letting her mind take indecent liberties with a man who could scarcely contain his dislike of her!

She concentrated on the scenery. The great plains were slowly giving way to more mountainous terrain. Boulders cropped up like great gray pigeons huddled

against the earth. Scraggly spruce began yielding to out-
bursts of pine and quaking aspen.

"Aren't those bright red flowers dotting the hillside
Indian Paint Brush? Isn't there a legend behind them?"
she asked, venturing into what she assumed was safe
territory.

Mindful of his mother's undying belief in the old
legends as well as her penchant for those fragile blos-
soms, Judson felt the question touch a sensitive chord
deep inside him. He was angered that that which held
deep spiritual significance for him was nothing more
than frivolous small talk to this outlander.

"It's symbolic of the red man's blood shed by the
whites when you stole our land," he snapped. "You
can read all about it in one of the books you bought to
brush up on Wyoming folklore. Most outsiders are sure
they can find all they'll need to know about the natives
in the library."

Stung by the cold fury of his words, Carrie eyed him
critically. How dare he make her feel like some kind of
cultural squatter!

"If I'm going to teach here, I'd like to be as knowl-
edgeable as possible," she replied woodenly in defense
of herself.

Judson raked his fingers through his dark hair and
sighed in exasperation. A man of few words who en-
joyed his solitude, he found superficial chitchat a waste
of energy. Certain that a litter of kittens would prove
less curious than this contrary female, he decided it was
time to put a stop to her endless questions.

"Are you going to ask me the name of every plant
and animal in the Wind River Mountain Range?"

"Maybe," she said, gracing him with an acerbic
smile.

Grudgingly Judson acknowledged how a smile could transform the uptight schoolteacher beside him into a lovely woman. Carrie Raben was something all buttoned up, he decided, and wondered just what kind of a man it would take to get those buttons undone. Aroused at the thought, he grimly reminded himself of the cost of such yearnings.

Nonetheless the young woman's interest in the native flora and fauna evoked in him something that at last put the two of them on peaceable terms: his love of this untamed land.

The further away from the city they traveled, the less Judson resembled a cornered mountain lion. As he pointed out coyotes and deer and red-tailed hawks, Carrie was impressed both by the depth of his knowledge and his uncanny eye. Where she could discern only landscape, he unerringly uncovered camouflaged wildlife. Clearly this man was on a spiritual plane with his fellow creatures. Knowledge tempered by respect and reverence was evident in the way his eyes held this vast wilderness that he called home, and Carrie found herself wondering if any woman would ever be able to compete with such a rival.

In a cloud of dust they passed a weathered, old gold mine claiming "The Carissa" as its name. Rounding the top of the next hill, Carrie was astonished to find herself in the midst of an actual ghost town. Little more than an outcropping of historic buildings, Atlantic City was still functioning—in a desolate, halfhearted sort of way.

"Almost there," Judson said, pulling up in front of the local mercantile. "Time to stop for lunch."

Climbing out of the pickup, Carrie thought to herself that there could not be enough liquid refreshment in the old establishment to put out the fire inside her. She followed Judson through the swinging doors and into the past. A 1912 calendar hung on the wall along with a collection of mining relics. The smell of whiskey mingled with dust, and Carrie almost expected an old-time saloon girl to step out from behind the antique bar and offer her a shot of whiskey.

Judson ordered a hamburger platter, and Carrie did the same. Looking over the rim of the old preserving jar in which her soft drink was served, she studied him closely. In the vehicle she had been nervous and reserved. In the dimly lit mercantile she felt more at ease in scrutinizing her driver. His face was lined with the telltale signs of a life of hard work beneath the sun, and it seemed to Carrie that the harsh exposure to the elements had given him an aura of determination and dignity. The lines around his eyes belied the sun-squinted curiosity of looking so far to see so little in these wide open spaces. Slightly off center, his nose had been broken a time or two, and a ridge of scar tissue ran along his left jawbone. Clearly there was as much hard living as hard work written on Judson Horn's handsome face. This was definitely a man who knew his own mind.

He was slightly older than she had first thought. Perhaps it was his lean body that had initially duped her into thinking him to be less than ten years older than she. Or maybe those incredibly tight-fitting jeans had deceived her. Was it merely the unusual combination of blue eyes set against such dark skin that made the man so phenomenally attractive? Or the sense that no woman would ever be able to tame him?

When her eyes fell upon that all-knowing smile of his, Carrie quickly diverted her gaze to a whimsical-looking creature hanging upon the wall. It was a rabbit with a set of horns growing from its head.

Judson's eyes twinkled with devilment, and a wicked thought played with the corners of his mouth. A harmless little practical joke would illustrate far more eloquently than he himself could the need to send the new teacher back where she belonged.

"It's a jackalope," he offered in explanation.

Ignoring the tug at his conscience, Judson quickly reminded himself that this delicate woman was simply not the right person for this job. It was a damned shame that Ted Cadenas had been forced into early retirement by a heart attack. With school starting in less than a week, the board members had jumped on the only application they had received like a trout upon the first mayfly of the season. They'd summarily dismissed Judson's concern that a city-bred girl would be unable to handle the elements and the isolation of the job.

"They're thick around here—and mean," he continued, warming to his subject. "If you see any around the schoolyard, just get out your shotgun and blast 'em. They've been known to gore children if they happen to come between a mama and her bunnylopes."

If Judson noticed her skepticism, he didn't show it. He was too busy cursing himself for falling headlong into eyes the color of a mountain meadow. Hotly he told himself that his desire to see Ms. Raben on an airplane heading in the opposite direction had less to do with the pooling of desire in his loins than the certainty that, with typical Anglo obstinacy, she would force her urban prejudices onto his children.

"They can carry tularemia—a nasty, contagious disease that you nor your schoolchildren would care to contract. First you bloat up and then—''

Not wanting to hear all the gruesome details, Carrie cut him off. "Surely blasting the little creatures is a little harsh?'' she questioned, envisioning herself pointing a shotgun out a window and blowing a chunk out of the hillside.

"Oh, well, if you're squeamish..." Judson rubbed his chin thoughtfully. "I guess I could show you how to trap the little buggers if you'd like. That way you won't ruin the fur, and if you skin 'em, you can collect a bounty for the pelts.''

The expression on Carrie's face indicated that option was not exactly palatable, either.

"You really...think it's...necessary to kill them?'' she asked.

"I sure do,'' he said, leaning forward and taking one of her hands into his.

A jolt surged through Carrie at his touch. The man's hands were rugged and callused and big. And when they enveloped hers, a sweet pain unlike any she had ever known before rushed through her. She could liken it only to grabbing hold of a live electrical wire and being unable to let go. Carrie couldn't help but wonder if a woman would feel the need to struggle beneath such rough hands...

Pushing himself away from the table, Judson picked up the bill and ambled over to the cash register. As she cast a lingering look around the ancient mercantile, Carrie heard Judson tell the cashier to throw in a length of rope for trapping jackalopes.

His sudden kindness left her feeling beholden, and she felt a rush of gratitude for his concern.

Opening the door into the bright sunshine, Judson Horn warned gruffly, "Remember, I warned you. Harmony ain't near so fancy.''

Chapter Two

Carrie's first impression of her new home was that it was a picture-perfect postcard. Nestled into the fringe of an aspen grove, the school overlooked a meadow speckled with purple lupine and enough wild sunflowers to give the impression that the entire countryside was dotted with butter. Threading its way though the meadow like a silver ribbon was the magnificent Popo Agie River.

A world unto itself, the tiny school district of Harmony, Wyoming, combined the old and the new. It consisted of a little white schoolhouse, complete with a bell in the steeple, which looked like it was taken straight out of a historical novel. A dirt field beside the buildings served as a playground providing two slides, swings, a merry-go-round and a wobbly basketball hoop nailed onto a pole. Beside the playground, a trailer house was set on a concrete foundation, and there, glistening beneath the sun in front of the two buildings, sat a shiny, new black-and-red Chevy pickup.

Eager to inspect it all for herself, Carrie flung the door open and hopped out of the dilapidated Ford pickup before it even rolled to a stop. She hurried up the weathered steps of the schoolhouse to impatiently jiggle the doorknob. It seemed to her that Judson Horn was taking his own sweet time getting out of the pickup.

Joining her at last on the narrow stoop, he drawled, "You're sure in a big hurry to be disappointed."

Carrie's resentment flared at the gloomy prediction. "I'll be the judge of how I feel, thank you."

Tapping her foot upon the smoothly worn wood, she added in a rush, "Now would you please be so kind as to open this door and let me in?"

His long, drawn-out sigh made it clear that he preferred to keep her locked out indefinitely. Carrie watched in shameless fascination while he fished the depths of his jeans' front pocket for the key. The blood throbbing inside her veins began to simmer, heightening the warm flush on her cheeks. This man was so utterly, so totally, sensual that she had little doubt he was aware of the effect he had upon her, on all women for that matter. The only difference being that Carrie was determined to resist him. She had no intention of becoming another in what was likely a long, long line of conquests. Besides, only a couple of months ago she had sworn off all men—especially good-looking ones with attitudes as big as their ten-gallon hats.

"Here you go," Judson said, handing over a silver ring linking four tarnished keys and a tacky plastic tab faintly marked with the school district's emblem.

Fervently Carrie hoped that they were keys that would lock out the heartache of the past as well as open the doors to the future. Not unlike a child on Christmas morning, she slipped the key into the lock and opened the schoolhouse door.

Had Judson Horn, the indomitable curmudgeon, not been there beside her she would have rushed to the front of the room and spun around in her excitement. Instead Carrie stood silently beside him in the doorway and wrapped her arms around herself.

It was like turning a page in a history book. Though the dozen desks were fairly new and there was a computer in the back of the room, Carrie felt exactly as if she had walked back into the nineteenth century. All the desks faced front, toward an old oak desk that appeared as immovable as history itself. On top of it rested an old battered school bell that had undoubtedly called to generations of children. Directly behind the teacher's desk was an expanse of antique slate board. Portraits of Washington and Lincoln graced the side walls as patriotically as they had throughout the century, and an American flag hung limply in the stillness of time. A potbellied stove dominated the back of the room. The fat potentate seemingly awaiting the time its fiery temperament would once again be stoked.

The deep timber of Judson's voice pulled her back into the twentieth century. "Well?"

Expecting a list of grievances as long as a trail drive, he braced himself against the door frame.

"It's perfect," she murmured. "Absolutely perfect!"

A flash of derision quickly replaced the momentary surprise that registered in Judson's eyes.

"We'll see how you feel when it's forty below, the power's out, and you've got to get a fire going in that old stove."

Damn it all, but she sure was pretty all lit up from the inside out that way. The look of genuine excitement shining in Carrie's soft green eyes touched a chord deep inside him. Her response was not at all what he had expected. He'd figured all he would have to do to run off this prissy Easterner would be to show her the primitive conditions of her contract, and she'd be history faster than he could say *adios*. It hadn't taken but the threat of hard times to send Cheryl Sue scurrying back into her daddy's big house, leaving him with a scarred back and a heart to match—not to mention a matched set of newborn twins.

Given his past history, Judson found the new schoolteacher to be most perplexing. Nervous, brash, frightened, spunky—an enigma all wrapped up in an appealing feminine package that spelled trouble with a capital *T!*

His icy gaze raked her face. "Come on," he muttered, reminding himself that he'd had enough trouble with women to last him a lifetime. "Let's put your luggage in the trailer."

Sinking into the soft earth with each step she took, Carrie followed after him, awkwardly maneuvering the short distance in her high-heel shoes. What was fashionable in Chicago, she realized with chagrin, was purely impractical in the Wind River Mountains of Wyoming.

"Welcome to paradise," he quipped, holding out one arm as if formally admitting her to Buckingham Palace.

Carrie was beginning to truly resent the man whose outlook on life was as clouded as the dirty windows in her new home. On the spot she decided that her very first item of business would be to clean those filmy windows. Too bad, she thought, Judson Horn's negative attitude couldn't be as easily wiped away.

A musty smell assailed her nostrils the instant she

stepped inside the trailer. Looking around the room,
Carrie decided it would have gratified the most austere
monk. The furniture consisted of a cheap couch and
matching chair. The windows had no curtains, and the
carpet was a sickly color of rust in which the major
traffic patterns were clearly and indelibly worn. Her
thoughts traveled back to her plush apartment in Chicago. Complete with tennis courts and swimming pool,
it had been chic, modern and *clean.*

Her parents would be horrified to find her living in
what they would surely consider squalor. Her mother
wouldn't so much as unpack her bags for an overnight
stay in a place like this. Feeling Judson's probing eyes
upon her, Carrie defiantly tipped up her chin, refusing
him the satisfaction of witnessing a single tear shed in
disappointment.

As he took a seat in the living room, Carrie began
her inspection. Following the narrow hallway to its end,
she opened the door to her bedroom. "Spartan" was
the word that came to mind. There was a bed with a
white chenille spread that had yellowed to a dingy shade
of beige, a small closet and a flimsy bureau. It struck
her as peculiar that such an austere decor failed to re-
press a fleeting, sinful fantasy of being alone with a
blue-eyed Indian stretched out across this bed....

Suddenly the room grew stiflingly hot. What in the
world was she doing fantasizing about a man who
clearly regarded her as an unwelcome interloper? Lest
Judson Horn become impatient, come looking for her
and find her engaged in a lustful fantasy that featured
him buck-naked on her bed, Carrie hastened back to the
living room.

There she was made aware of how very long Judson's
legs were as she was forced to step over them. Sitting

in the chair with his hands behind his head, he looked as comfortable as a cat that called the world his own domain. And as Carrie felt his eyes run the length of her, she had the unnerving feeling that if she wasn't careful, she might just wind up being this dangerous tom's next meal.

"There's no phone," he informed her as nonchalantly as she imagined he would relay the going price of beef on the hoof. "Since it's not worth the phone company's time and equipment to run a line all the way out here for just one trailer, you have to go back to Atlantic City to place a call. You'll probably want to invest in a cellular phone for your own personal use, but in case of emergencies, there's a two-way radio."

Rising smoothly from the chair, he walked into the kitchen, pulled an ancient-looking apparatus from the narrow pantry and proceeded to explain the operations of two-way communication.

This was far more primitive than Carrie had ever imagined. The term could just as easily be applied to the man standing beside her. Filling her lungs with the heady scent of his musky masculinity, she found it increasingly difficult to keep her mind focused on the task at hand.

"Knowing how to work this radio could mean the difference between life and death," he said in a tone Carrie suspected was reserved especially for ridiculous city slickers like herself.

Keenly aware of the woman next to him, Judson battled a sudden overwhelming feeling of protectiveness for his children's teacher. He knew he intimidated her, meant to in fact, so why did the widening of those great big eyes make him feel like such a beast? The feeling threatened to put a chink in his well-polished emotional armor. She was so utterly vulnerable standing there looking up at him as if he were an encyclopedia of Western living that for a minute he almost wished he could be the white-hatted cowboy she wanted him to be. The irony of that particular image brought an off-kilter smirk to Judson's lips. As he recalled, in the movies the good guys were usually fair-skinned blonds. Breeds were generally cast in roles several pegs below the black-hatted villain.

Distracted by the erotic curve of Carrie's lower lip held in consternation between her teeth, Judson was seized by a sudden urge to brush those feathery bangs away from her sweet, open face. How in the name of hell could a spoiled Eastern brat possibly arouse such tender feelings in him?

Was it that perfume she wore, a subtle blend of flowers and musk, that tempted him to disregard the mistakes of the past and recklessly indulge in the possibilities of the moment? Angrily, Judson reminded himself that no fragrance was powerful enough to cover the stench of prejudice. He was no longer a schoolboy to be won over by the batting of long eyelashes and the promise of happily-ever-afters that ultimately disintegrated beneath public scrutiny. That lesson was permanently etched upon his back.

The problem, Judson told himself, was simply that he was a warm-blooded man who had been a long time without a woman's touch. Apparently far too long. Maybe it was time to reconsider sexy Estelle Hanway's unconditional standing invitation into her bed. If that were the case, he wondered why the thought held even less appeal than usual today.

Deliberately he inserted a cool tone of indifference in his voice. "After I show you to your winter transportation, you'll need to go into town to buy some supplies. Other than a few conveniences at the gas station, Atlantic City doesn't have anything in the way of groceries so Lander's your best choice. And I'd suggest you stock up on canned goods. You won't get many chances to run to town, and there's always the possibility of an early September snow. I'd hate for you to starve to death during a blizzard.''

Carrie doubted it. For some inexplicable reason the man seemed to despise her. That way he had of looking right through her made her feel as insignificant as a gnat, and she had the feeling that he would, in fact, be elated by the thought of her frozen demise.

Mutely, she followed him outside to a spot behind the trailer.

Pointing at a dusty heap, Judson calmly disclosed, ''That's how you get out in the winter.''

Covered with a tarp and a layer of dust sat a massive snowmobile.

''You've got to be kidding!''

Carrie could no more envision herself astride this monstrosity than she could see herself climbing atop a raging bull. She was as stunned by the fact that she was going to have to somehow learn how to drive this formidable contraption as she was by the tremendous amount of wood stacked against the backside of the schoolhouse. Surely it was excessive. The winters couldn't possibly be as severe as this infuriating man would lead her to believe.

Judson didn't have to say a word. That I-told-you-so look of his said it all loud and clear.

Pushing his hat back on his head, he regarded her as a little lamb lost. When he informed her that it was time for him to get going, Carrie merely looked at him blankly in response. He felt compelled to add in explanation as he turned to go, "Look, I've got a date, but if you want to, you can follow me into Lander. It's the nearest town from here."

Judson deliberately withheld the fact that his "date" was nothing more than picking up his children. He wasn't exactly sure why he didn't want Carrie knowing just how unattached he was—that he couldn't even remember the last time he had been on a real date. But he decided if the way his libido was presently holding his brain hostage was any indication, it was definitely time to remedy that. Preferably with a woman who had zero expectations of any commitment. There were only two things in this world that Judson Horn was truly committed to. And right now he was half an hour late picking them up from the baby-sitter's.

Carrie felt as if she had been sucker-punched. She blamed her reaction less on the fact that this handsome cowboy was involved in a relationship than on the realization that he was heading right toward that beautiful red-and-black pickup. The instant she had seen it parked in front of the school, she had assumed that the brand-new vehicle was the transportation provided in her contract. That it, in fact, belonged to Judson could only mean that the old bomber in which she had been driven here was to be hers.

Swallowing her disappointment, Carrie stammered, "Th-that's all right. I want to get settled in. You go on, and don't worry about me... But before you go...could you possibly..."

It pained her to have to ask Judson for help, but although she was initially skeptical about the horned menace, her introduction to myriad new fauna had Carrie worried that the area was indeed teeming with exotic perils.

"There's, uh, that little matter of those jackalopes..."

At the reminder, Judson's face broke into a wide grin. "Oh, that's right, I forgot," he said, snapping his fingers. "Wait here just a minute. I'll be right back."

Just what *was* it about that crooked smile that made her heart thump so frantically? Conscious of the quiver in her stomach, Carrie watched him saunter over to the pickup. Unable to tear her eyes away from his snug jeans, she told herself that it was ridiculous for her to be feeling this way. Aside from the fact that the last thing she needed right now in her life was *any* romantic attachment, this particular man had made it quite clear that he not only didn't like her much, he was dating someone else. Judging by those drop-dead good looks, she wouldn't have been surprised if he had an entire harem at his disposal.

Plainly, Judson Horn was off limits, and that was all there was to that. Thank God and good riddance to any future heartache.

Returning momentarily with rope in hand, he began fastidiously fashioning a snare. Fascinated by the sight of rough hemp manipulated by his strong, masculine hands, Carrie felt her mouth grow dry.

Realizing that this would be something she herself would be expected to master, she asked with a shaky sigh, "Would you mind teaching me how to do that?"

"Not at all."

That lazy, irresistible grin instantly disarmed her, spreading warmth throughout her body and leaving a hot blush upon her cheeks. Surely that trademark smile had won him many a skirmish! As Judson reached around her and began guiding the rope through her fingers, Carrie swallowed a sharp intake of air. Trapped in his arms and surrounded by his woodsy scent, she could feel the shivers tripping up and down her spine. Though her mind urged her to run away, her body seemed powerless to obey.

"Think you can manage that?" he asked, pulling the rope into a small noose.

Was he crazy? How could he expect her to pay attention when her heart was racing a hundred miles a minute and her thoughts were concentrated on the muscles corded along his forearms? Such strong arms, she thought absently, were made to make a woman feel protected and cherished.

Say something, her mind urged. But she was unable to fill her lungs with enough air to expel a single syllable. What was it about this man's touch that instantly turned her brains to pudding?

Staring down at their joined hands, she asked at last, "Would you mind showing me one more time?" Try as she might, Carrie was unable to make her voice register louder than a whisper.

"Not at all."

Giving in to the urge, Judson bent so that his mouth was next to her ear. Whether he personally liked her or not, there was no denying that Carrie Raben felt damned good in his arms. Her waist was so incredibly small he wondered if it were possible to span its circumference with his two hands. He had little doubt that if the severe winter and isolation of the outback didn't get lovely Ms. Raben, some rich, lonely rancher would. Just off the top of his head, he could think of at least a dozen eligible fellows who would give their left arm for the chance of snapping up such a sweet, cultured morsel. Knowing how fast word traveled in Harmony, he figured there would be a line of beaus outside her trailer door before his dust had had a chance to settle.

For some reason that he couldn't quite put his finger on, Judson found the thought strangely unsettling. He told himself it was just because that could leave his children without a teacher right in the middle of the year when it would be next to impossible to find a replacement. Still, when Carrie raised her lowered eyelashes to meet his searching look, Judson knew for certain that it was he, not the children of Harmony, who was in trouble.

Suddenly he couldn't remember what had prompted him to even consider pulling this sweet, young thing's leg. The naiveté shimmering in those wide green eyes resurrected in him a streak of chivalry that he thought had died long ago at the end of a whip.

Carrie's hair felt soft against his cheek, her subtle fragrance bewitched him, and a perfectly graphic sensual image flitted across his mind as he trailed the rope across her pale, slim wrists. Repeating his instructions, he couldn't help but wonder just exactly what kind of a trap it was that he was setting.

Carrie suspected that her heartbeat galloping at breakneck speed was a dead giveaway to the fact that she was a woman without a man in her life. Glad that he was unable to witness the crimson flush of her face, she tried her damnedest to block out the effect that Judson's closeness was having upon her. When at last she was able to master the process of setting a snare herself, she stepped and surveyed her handiwork.

"Simple task for an ex-Girl Scout!" she quipped, self-consciously making light of her racing pulse.

Leaning against the side of the old schoolhouse, Judson decreed with a definite sparkle in his eye, "Who'da thought a greenhorn could set such a fine jackalope snare?"

Confused by a sudden rush of pleasure at the compliment, Carrie was startled by how warmly his words filled the hollow inside her. Perhaps she had been wrong about this man after all. Perhaps her first impression of him had been too hastily formed. Perhaps it was only the rigors of hard living that made him seem so distant and solitary. Perhaps she needed to have her head examined.

Feeling the need to put some distance between them, Carrie said with newfound assurance, "I'll set a couple out a ways."

Picking up a length of rope, she stepped off into the high grass surrounding the playground. She had gone less than ten paces when a pair of brawny arms grabbed her around the waist and lifted her off the ground. A red haze of panic descended over her as her mind filled with dreadful possibilities.

"Let me go!" Carrie yelled, resisting him for all she was worth. Her high heels connected with a shinbone, and an oath echoed against mountain walls.

Judson stumbled backward, dropping her upon the hard dirt. Carrie scrambled to her feet, but Judson was already loping toward his vehicle. Helplessly she watched as he pulled something out from under the seat. When he turned to face her, a pistol dangled from his hand.

It seemed incongruous to her that this man would want to hurt her, but having dealt with violence on a daily basis in her previous school, she wasn't taking any chances. Her mind raced to come up with a way to make this lunatic see reason. She remembered her instructor's words from a self-defense class she had taken. *If you can, engage your attacker in conversation. Make him see you as an individual.* Certainly there was no chance of some kindly police officer intervening way out here in the boonies.

"Wait a minute... P-please..." she stammered, backing slowly away.

But Judson wasn't listening. Expressionless, he looked right through her. Raising the gun to shoulder height, he steadied his grip with his free hand and shattered the silence with a squeeze of the trigger. Carrie heard the bullet whiz past her and compelled her eyes to follow the direction of the smoking barrel.

There, curled up in the long grass just a step away from her discarded length of rope lay a huge gray and yellow diamond-patterned snake. Though decapitated, its body kept coiling and winding, doubling and falling back on itself. Fearing the still-groping tail could somehow find her and wrap itself around her, Carrie stepped back.

Judson holstered his gun. Then he rubbed his raw shin.

"What in the hell's the matter with you? Are you deaf and blind both?" he demanded, the look in his eyes illuminating his doubts about the new schoolteacher's mental stability.

"You scared me!" she snapped in her defense.

The woman was a master of understatement. The terror glistening in her eyes reminded Judson of a fawn cornered by a pack of wolves. What had he done to make her come to such unflattering conclusions about his intentions? Bothered by the question, he told himself that it was enough just knowing that the district had entered into a nine-month contract with a crazy woman.

One whose innate prejudices conjured up a bad B-movie fantasy based on the old preconceptions of what savage Indians did to white women. His eyes narrowed in cold fury.

Limping over to the dead snake, he picked it up by the tail and held it at arm's length. Reaching into his hip pocket, he pulled out a knife and sliced off its rattles—ten to be exact. Stepping toward her, he shook his closed fist next to Carrie's ear. As innocent as a baby's rattle, it was indeed the sound of death.

"Whenever you hear this sound, stop and back away slowly. Rattlesnakes, not Indians, are the real threat out here, lady."

Tossing the snake into the bushes, he added coldly, "One more step and we'd be having this conversation at the hospital."

Judson's words clicked inside Carrie's head like the rattles of that diamond-backed snake lying dead beneath the afternoon sun. She battled the sudden flush that swept over her. It was a sensation that had little to do with the heat of the day and everything to do with the man who stood looking at her as if he should be helping her into a straitjacket. The rustling of aspen leaves seemed quite far away as terror drained from her body and the ground swayed precariously under her feet.

"You're not going to faint, are you?" he asked, holding out both arms to catch her just in case.

Guilt pressed upon Judson's heart like a grinding stone. It appeared he'd scared the poor thing to death.

Valiantly trying to insert a hardy tone into her voice, Carrie responded, "I've never fainted in my life." *But there's always a first time for everything...*

Struggling to regain her senses was like trying to find her way up from the bottom of a deep mountain lake.

No, make that the depths of a pair of blue eyes filled with what appeared to be genuine concern. What was happening to her? A minute ago she was fighting this man with all her might, and now she was leaning against him for support, practically begging him to wrap those strong, sensuous arms around her again.

Putting both hands on his chest, Carrie woozily attempted to steady herself against that impenetrable wall and recover a modicum of her dignity.

Judson derived little satisfaction in being right about this rough country being no place for one so fragile. Damn it, shouldn't being right feel better? Looking into Carrie's pale, delicate face, he was reminded of his children. Perfect angels—when sleeping. And like his twins, she evoked in him a fierce possessiveness and the irrational desire to keep her safe forever.

Judson's body, however, reacted in a manner that was far from fatherly. He was excruciatingly aware of Carrie's soft curves against his hard, lean frame. Her nipples were taut through soft silk; his arousal just as obvious through rough demin. If he didn't get the hell out of here right now, he might as well hand her the knife to cut out his heart.

Good Lord! Just how many times did a man need to be horsewhipped to learn a lesson? The muscle along his jaw bunched at the memory.

Holding on to her by both elbows, Judson took a step back then let his arms fall loosely at his sides.

Bewildered, Carrie stood in front of him trembling like a butterfly, riveted to this singular spot of the spinning globe by the warmth centered deep inside her. This was definitely not the way she had intended to start the school year—in the arms of a blue-eyed Native American who had made it quite clear he didn't even particularly like her!

What must he think about her now that she had literally thrown herself into his arms? In a community as isolated as Harmony, it couldn't take much to set tongues wagging.

"Are you gonna be all right?" Judson asked, his voice a sexy, agitated purr that sent her imagination traveling down a road clearly marked Danger—Enter At Your Own Risk!

Swallowing hard, Carrie simply nodded.

Apparently unconvinced, Judson ran a work-roughened fingertip beneath her chin and tilted her face up. Beneath his close inspection, twin roses bloomed upon her cheeks.

Certain the most passionate kiss could not have been more erotic than the tenderness in that one callused finger, Carrie felt her knees grow as weak as a baby's. She hated herself for blushing again. It was the Raben curse—fair skin that acted as a barometer for every emotion and rendered her absolutely useless in a game of poker.

Seemingly satisfied at last that she wasn't going to collapse and melt into a puddle of estrogen at his feet, Judson turned abruptly on his heels. Following after him like a scolded pup, Carrie heard the gravel crunch beneath his feet as he reached his pickup and jerked open the door.

Climbing behind the wheel, he tossed her a gruff directive. "By the way, if you don't have one, you'd better think about gettin' yourself a gun."

"But I don't believe in guns," she stated unequivocally.

Judging by his reaction, Carrie was certain a kick in

the stomach would have had a less negative effect than this particular admission. Judson's eyes glinted dangerously, making her feel at once both vulnerable and foolish.

"What you don't seem to understand," he continued, speaking slowly as if English were not her native tongue, "is that our children need someone not just to teach them but to protect them, as well. There may come a time you'll need a gun, say, to clear off the front steps of some such unfriendly critter as a rattlesnake or a bear."

Carrie suppressed a shudder at the thought.

"Look, no one would blame you if you decide that you're just not cut out for this job." Pausing a moment to wipe the sweat from beneath the brim of his black Stetson hat, Judson Horn looked unflinchingly into her eyes. "Quite frankly, it would save us all a lot of grief if you'd make that decision right now instead of midterm when it will be damned near impossible to find a replacement. Out here it's a matter of survival."

His words pierced Carrie's heart like the rows of barbed wire that lined the road to Harmony. He was right, of course. She had come out West naively expecting to leave heartache and urban crime behind only to be greeted by a rattlesnake in her front yard! Still Carrie could not allow herself to be so quickly deterred. What she had left behind had been a different kind of wilderness, and she knew that if she kept running away from her fears she would ultimately destroy herself in the process.

"I'm staying," she said with sudden resolution.

Whether it was disgust or admiration reflected in Judson Horn's eyes, Carrie wasn't sure. She knew only that she was done running and that she was determined to make Harmony her home.

"Suit yourself," Judson said, his expression a studied mask of indifference. Reaching into the glove compartment, he pulled out an envelope with her name typed upon it and handed it to her through the open window.

With that, Judson tipped his hat and threw the pickup into gear.

Something in that simple gesture made Carrie's heart beat more quickly. She couldn't quite put her finger on it, but there was something undefinably sexy about that damned cowboy hat.

As dust rose about the receding vehicle, she noticed that Judson Horn didn't so much as glance back.

She was on her own.

Chapter Three

School was to start in less than a week, and she didn't know where to begin. First there was enough house cleaning in both buildings to keep her busy for a month. Then there was the fact that she wasn't sure how to organize one schoolroom to accommodate eighteen children at six different grade levels. Still, those worries would have to be temporarily put aside. Right now food was her most imminent problem. Aware that the half a hamburger she'd eaten in Atlantic City wouldn't last her long, she realized that somehow she was going to have to get comfortable driving a beat-up, old stick shift— and fast.

Sinking to the front steps of the schoolhouse, Carrie felt the tears spill down her face. The surprising thing was that they weren't tears of self-pity but rather of unexpected joy. Beneath the never-ending Wyoming sky, she felt spiritually cleansed. The sun filtered through the quaking aspen, splaying exquisite patterns upon the ground. The air she breathed was sweet and clean. The rippling of the river and the rustling of the leaves seemed to her the most soothing sounds on earth.

High above two eagles circled, brushing wing tips on clouds before separating and going their own ways. A sharp pain ripped through Carrie as she was reminded of the engagement she had severed back in Chicago. From the very start she had worried about the possible consequences of mixing business with pleasure. Never get involved with the boss, she had told herself, but Scott Ballson insisted that the fact that he was her principal had nothing to do with their out-of-school relationship. He assured her that their private lives were their own.

Then again, Carrie reminded herself bitterly, he had also told her he'd back her a hundred percent. In truth, Scott had stood behind her only long enough to stab her in the back.

"Just because I changed a student's grade?" he had sputtered incredulously, staring at the engagement ring she had pressed into his palm. "I can't believe you're acting so childishly."

"It's a matter of betrayal."

"It's a matter of politics," he had scoffed, alluding to the fact that Cindy Lawton's father was on the school board and that the failing mark the senior had earned in Carrie's class not only rendered her ineligible to play in the state basketball tournament but also jeopardized the pretty senior's graduation, as well. When Carrie had adamantly refused Scott's request to raise the grade, he exercised the "administrative privilege" of changing it himself—without her consent or knowledge.

"I hate to be the one to burst your bubble, Carrie, but it's the way of the world. Everyone does it."

"I don't," she had said with conviction.

"Excuse me," Scott had added maliciously, "I meant to say it's important to anyone who wants to keep a job in education... And that just happens to be me. Have you ever thought how *your* obstinacy might endanger *my* job?"

As usual, Scott was able to twist things around so that she was the one left feeling guilty. He was able to temporarily smooth things over, but Carrie felt uneasy about her decision to reconsider breaking off their engagement. Uneasy enough that when she was in the girls' bathroom one day and accidentally overheard Cindy talking to a friend, she neither plugged her ears nor stepped out from behind the stall to identify herself.

"How *did* you get that grade changed in Miss Raben's class? She's such a stickler about eligibility," asked a shrill, bubble-popping voice through the metal stall door.

"Easy," came a laughing reply.

For a moment Carrie feared the girl's explanation would be drowned out by the gurgle of water splashing in a sink.

"I just gave our horny principal a little of what his goody-two-shoes fiancée's been holding out on. Can you imagine anyone being a virgin at *her* age?"

The wind that roared through Carrie's entire being threatened to blow her spirit away like a dry reed. Her desecration was complete. She didn't know which was worse—to be so completely duped by a man who would stoop so low as to abuse his position or to be made to feel a freak by a loose teenager willing to demean herself for so little in return.

After a heartfelt cry that lasted the better part of her planning period, Carrie had marched straight out of the bathroom and into Scott's office. When confronted, he'd vehemently protested her accusation, but his initial expression belied the truth. Carrie's resignation followed the next day. As well as the reason why mailed to every member of the school board.

Scott was outraged, dangerously so. And Carrie felt certain he would have made good his threat to do her bodily harm as well as keep her from ever getting another teaching job altogether had she not discovered a listing in the placement bulletin indicating Harmony School District was anxious to fill this last minute position. A follow-up call confirmed they were, in fact, desperate.

The experience left her sour on all men. The safest course of action, Carrie decided, was to simply assume they all were creeps until proven otherwise. She certainly didn't need to be kicked by the same mule twice to know that she would never risk her heart and her pride like that again with any man—let alone one in a position of authority over her. No way, never again.

Watching the pair of eagles seek opposite ends of the horizon, Carrie knew if she could ever truly begin the healing process, it would be beneath this unending blue sky. The exact color of Judson Horn's eyes, it defied a paintbrush.

Slipping a fingernail beneath an edge of the tear-spattered envelope that he had given her, Carrie slit it open. An invitation for a districtwide ice cream social fell into her lap.

She smiled.

Hope rested gently on her shoulder like a sparrow. All alone in the world for the first time in her life, she was surprised how very much she liked the feeling.

On his way out of Harmony, Jud swerved to miss a gray tabby cat that had darted out in front of his pickup.

He chastised himself for almost getting himself killed just because something in that wild cat's eyes reminded him of the woman he had just left behind. He couldn't get over the fact that she'd actually fallen for that old chestnut about jackalopes. Telling himself that the silly woman deserved whatever she got, Jud figured that if a good dose of humility hastened her departure, he was, after all, only doing her a favor in the long run. Still, something haunting in the youthful schoolteacher's naïveté pulled at his conscience.

Muttering an oath, Judson threw on the brakes and flipped a U-turn in the middle of the road. All the way back up that dusty road, he swore at his own soft heart. Of course, the virtuous thing to do was to go back and tell her the truth about the mythical jackalope before it ended up causing her any real embarrassment. Although he knew she'd be spitting mad to discover he'd been joshing her, for some inexplicable reason Judson preferred she hear it from him rather than from someone else. Assuming that she was probably just now coming to terms with the terrible mistake she'd made and was in need of comforting, he prepared himself to find the new schoolteacher bawling her pretty little eyes out.

But what he found awaiting him in the school yard upon his return was something else entirely. There on the merry-go-round spun a very undignified, uninhibited maiden. Carrie's jacket, high heels and nylons lay neatly stacked on the hood of the old pickup as she clung tightly to the merry-go-round bar and leaned far back to stare up at the cloudless sky. Her hair swished softly in the breeze as she whirled around and around, oblivious to the fact that she was not alone.

The sight took Judson's breath away. He was simultaneously filled with pure, unmitigated lust and the desire to momentarily abandon his adult responsibilities and join this enchantress astride the merry-go-round.

"Just a kid herself," he whispered to himself.

Reluctant to honk the horn and make his presence known, Judson was quick to assure himself that there really wasn't any reason why the truth couldn't wait another day. Backing silently down the road, he tried to erase from his mind the image of Carrie Raben playing on a merry-go-round. Unfortunately it proved as indelible and stirring as the memory of her lithe body pressed against his.

After indulging in her bit of playground fun, Carrie set about the business of moving in. She attacked the dirt and grime of her new home with the vengeance of a crusader. She was sure she had burned up more energy than in any of her costly aerobic classes. By mid-afternoon, she was ready for a break. Offering silent thanksgiving to her father for insisting she learn how to drive on a stick shift when she turned sixteen, Carrie crawled into the driver's seat of her old pickup and searched the contents of the glove box for a map. Luckily she found one. Although she was rusty, it quickly came back to her, and soon Carrie was bouncing down the washboardy road toward Lander where she purchased not only groceries but also a few things at the local department store to make her new home more livable.

She found the town as rustic and charming as Harmony itself. Populated with friendly, unpretentious people who made her feel right at home, Lander was a pleasant contrast to the fast-paced, impersonal atmosphere of the big city she had left behind. Carrie hoped this idyllic hideaway never underwent the crass commercialism of Aspen, Vail or Jackson Hole. As far as she was concerned, Carrie thought as she headed out of town, Lander was perfect just as it was.

By the time she had unpacked her supplies, made a plateful of brownies to take to the social and put the finishing touches to her decor, Carrie was exhausted.

Slipping between clean sheets that evening, she surveyed the results of her hard work with satisfaction. Elbow grease, new curtains and slipcovers had helped to transform her new home into a cheerful if not elegant spot to spend the next nine months.

She rose late the next morning and decided to start the day by indulging in a languid bubble bath and taking her time to get ready for the ice cream social. This would be her first opportunity before Open House to make a good first impression on her new boss and associates, and she was looking forward to making their acquaintance. Dressing with care, she chose a simple flowered sundress with a short white jacket to cover her bare shoulders.

On her way to her first small-town social, Carrie tried to use the forty-five-mile drive to Lander to collect her thoughts. But the prospect of seeing Judson Horn again sent her pulses leaping. What exactly was it about that man's eyes that defied a woman to break through that thin layer of ice to dive to the bottom of those blue, blue depths? Insanity, she wagered, recalling her promise to keep her distance from all men in the future.

Carrie arrived right on time at the park with a plate of brownies and a nervous smile. Surrounded by aged cottonwoods and traversed by a brook, Lander City Park was quaint and enchanting. Children climbed happily on the playground equipment as adults mingled around the picnic tables. She stopped momentarily to watch a tennis match between two athletic boys.

She and Scott had been a strong doubles team, and just watching a short volley made her feel suddenly melancholy. Gently, she reminded herself that it took more than a strong backhand and a killer serve to make a marriage. Strength of character and fidelity headed her list, although she would have been lying to say that sheer physical attraction wasn't right up there near the top, as well.

When Judson spied Carrie Raben standing forlornly beside the tennis courts, he felt his heart lurch unnaturally against his chest. She looked as pretty as a bouquet of mountain wildflowers. How was it that her looks seemed to grow on him each time he saw her?

"Whoa," he admonished himself, pulling hard on his own reins.

He recognized the feeling that welled up inside himself for what it was—pure, unadulterated lust. Judson shook his head in self-reproof. He hadn't been able to get Carrie Raben out of his head for more than a minute since he'd left her yesterday blithely playing on the merry-go-round. Assuring himself that it was simply residual guilt that he was feeling, Judson determined that the first matter of the afternoon would be to set matters straight between them. All things considered, it just might be a lot safer making the truth about the fictitious jackalope known in a public place.

A deep, resonant voice shattered Carrie's solitude, plunging her into a pair of clear blue eyes. Judson Horn was wearing jeans and a bright Western print shirt that snapped up the front. Shocked at the way her blood raced through her veins at the sight of him, Carrie attempted to insert a tone of nonchalance into her greeting.

"Hello," she said, uncomfortably aware that he was looking at her as if she were the most delectable sundae around.

"You look nice today," he drawled.

The compliment centered a tight ball of pleasure low in her stomach, which exploded, leaving warm spots of pink upon her cheeks.

"Thanks," she managed to say without stammering, and was rewarded with a slow, sexy smile that reached right inside her and heightened her already-keen sexual awareness of him.

Just then a hefty man wearing a blood-red tie approached with an outstretched hand and stepped between them. "You must be Carrie Raben," he beamed, pumping her hand up and down. "I'm Bill Madden. I interviewed you over the phone."

Grateful for the friendly ease with which her superintendent seemed to accept her, Carrie smiled warmly.

"Since you've already met the chairman," he said, pulling her over to a nearby group of people, "let me introduce you to the rest of the school board."

Chairman!

The word rang as loudly as a gunshot, and Carrie felt it hit her between her eyes as surely as if it had been a bullet.

Judson Horn was her boss!

Carrie couldn't believe her ears. What demented pleasure would anyone evoke in purposely leading her to believe he was merely a hired hand when he was, in fact, the chairman of the school board? How could she have ever deluded herself into thinking Judson Horn had a single redeeming quality? Wondering how this devil-in-no-disguise ever got himself elected to the school board in the first place, she somehow managed a gracious smile as her superintendent led her to the table where the other members of the board were seated.

As each stood to be formally introduced, Carrie sensed the amusement twinkling in Judson's azure eyes. Leaning his long body against an old cottonwood, it seemed obvious that he was enjoying her discomfiture immensely.

How I'd like to wipe that smirk off your handsome face... she thought to herself, extending her hand to a woman with a grin so wide she could have taken it off a jack-o'-lantern.

"Hi, my name's Snuffy. I'm your bus driver, and I deliver your mail, too."

Her broad smile revealed the reason for her peculiar name: a wad of chewing tobacco tucked neatly between her gum and bottom lip.

"Glad to meet you," Carrie said, taking a callused hand into her own. The older woman's grip was solid, her smile honest. Carrie liked her immediately.

"Afraid of being so far out all by yourself?" asked a bowlegged fellow whom Bill introduced as Ace. "Being nothing more than a schoolhouse and a trailer, Harmony can get to be a mighty lonesome place—especially in the winter when you can get snowed in. Those who aren't used to it tend to go stir-crazy."

Duly suspicious now, Carrie looked for a hint of derision in the rancher's weathered features, but all she could discern was genuine concern.

"I doubt if I'll go stir-crazy, but I might get a little homesick," she replied. And, as if to reassure the group that she was truly prepared for whatever emergency that might come up, added quickly, "I'll be fine once I get used to the area. I'm grateful to Mr. Horn for showing me how to set jackalope snares around the school. Now I'm sure I'll feel safe when I'm out scouting around on my own."

Carrie wasn't sure what she had said that caused the entire group to burst into laughter, but her cheeks flamed crimson just the same.

"Jackalope snares, you say?"

The question caused another roar of laughter.

"I'd like to market something like that myself!" someone said, slapping Judson on the back in an act of camaraderie.

Suppressing a chuckle himself, her superintendent hastened to explain. "I'm afraid you've been had, Carrie. There is no such thing as a jackalope. It's just a traditional Wyoming joke to get the tourists going and to make a few bucks."

Had a more perfect idiot ever been born? Carrie asked herself over the lump in her throat. So this is my initiation. Thank you so much for the warm Western welcome! Tipping up her chin defiantly, she turned to Judson Horn.

His chest tightened beneath her steady gaze. What had initially seemed purely comical now suddenly seemed mean-spirited. Outwardly the new school-teacher was handling all the joshing quite well, but he could easily read the betrayal glistening in those misty green eyes. He himself had long ago learned to control his body's reflexes so as to hide any sign of pain. The fact that Carrie wore hers so openly only served to deepen his sense of guilt. Despite that plastic smile plastered on her face, she looked ready to cry. Kicking himself for not divulging the truth as he had intended to do the other day, he truly regretted that her humiliation had been so very public.

For someone who had just pulled off the practical joke of the decade, Judson Horn felt like the biggest jerk on the face of the earth.

Pushing himself away from the tree, he attempted to explain quietly.

"I meant to tell you before—"

"Before I made such a complete fool of myself, Mr. Horn?"

"Oh, no—" interrupted Bill Madden, anxious to smooth over any tension between the two. "I wouldn't say that. In fact, I'd like to take this opportunity to tell you how impressed I am with the fact that you're such a good sport."

Her superintendent tried to soften the sting of her embarrassment by telling a story about how the jack-alope had recently caused an international furor when a group of Wyoming businessmen brought along stuffed jackalopes as a gift for some Asian dignitaries on a goodwill visit. They were stopped at customs where officials were certain the creatures should be on the endangered species list, and it took several hours to get somebody from the U.S. embassy to clear up the Wyomingites' practical joke.

Suffering through the next couple of hours, Carrie endured the ribbing she received from everyone including the janitor and the city mayor. Despite Bill's attempt at making light of her gullibility, the social Carrie had been so looking forward to had unfortunately proven to be far less "social" than she had anticipated. As far as she was concerned, the chairman of the board had effectively accomplished what he had set out to do—sabotage her first impression upon the small community.

Discreetly checking her watch, Carrie counted the minutes till she could slip quietly away. She thought no one noticed her collect her empty platter and head for the parking lot, but just as she was opening the door of her pickup to take her leave, she felt a hand upon her bare shoulder. Without looking up, she knew who it was. No one else in this world had such sexy, electric hands capable of setting her on fire and befuddling all her senses at once.

"Could you wait a minute?" Judson asked in a tone so deep and mellow it could qualify as a purr.

Removing the hand from her shoulder as if it were some sort of disgusting insect, Carrie responded dryly, "Sorry, I'm running late—got to rush home to check my traps for those treacherous jackalopes, you know."

Her withering glance seemed to bounce right off Judson's thick skull. In fact, the only effect her sarcasm seemed to have upon him was to deepen the dimples on both sides of his mouth.

"I'd be glad to help," he offered with a lopsided grin.

Ignoring the fact that he looked appealingly like a naughty little boy caught with his hand in the cookie jar, Carrie brushed him aside.

"You've *helped* more than enough already, thank you very much," she snapped, climbing into her pickup and slamming the door shut.

Tears pricked at the back of her eyelids. The absolute last thing she wanted to do was to let her new boss see her break down and cry. Peeling out of the parking lot, she was gratified to see the chairman of the board in her rearview mirror brushing dust from his black felt hat.

Carrie reprimanded herself for such a silly, juvenile

outburst. A woman who generally prided herself on her composure, she couldn't explain the effect Judson Horn had on her. Just because he was a class-one jerk didn't necessarily mean she had to go out of her way to alienate the man who would be signing her paychecks.

She was surprised at how deeply his treachery hurt. Despite the fact that Judson had made it quite clear from the first that he didn't think she belonged here, Carrie had nevertheless thought the man had felt a tiny measure of tenderness toward her.

Dismissing the ache in her heart as disgust toward all men in general, she told herself that it was truly a blessing the way things had worked out. Having solemnly sworn to never, ever again become romantically involved with another employer—particularly one who deliberately went out of his way to make her look like an idiot—Carrie was glad for a good reason to end those foolish fantasies that had plagued her since the first time she laid eyes on this workingman's cowboy.

Right now she assessed the chances of anything developing between her and that despicable practical joker as being on par with her chances of having the Sweepstake Prize Patrol waiting on her doorstep when she got home. Even if at some point in the distant future she could overcome the embarrassment of being so thoroughly duped, Carrie wouldn't make the same mistake again. She wasn't up to risking her heart anew, to any man, and especially not to a brooding loner who acted as if she had single-handedly brought smallpox into his ancestors' villages.

Still if there was any way of getting along with the chairman of the board, Carrie knew she would simply have to find it. One thing was for certain. She wasn't up to another year like Scott Ballson had just put her through. Neither her heart nor her career could stand it.

Chapter Four

Carrie looked out at the freshly scrubbed faces and excited, squirming bodies that filled the small schoolroom on the first day of school. She had prepared herself to encounter the same apathetic, hardened expressions that the children of Chicago public schools donned as a matter of daily armor. These sweet, eager faces looking expectantly up at her came as a complete surprise. Any one of them could easily adorn a cereal box touting old-fashioned Americanism.

To someone used to following a detailed, mandated curriculum it was disconcerting to obtain a class roster by simply passing around a piece of paper and having each child sign his name and grade. Carrie collected the class roster and studied the list. Two names jumped off the page: Brandy and Cowboy Horn, both in sixth grade.

Her heart skipped a beat.

"Cowboy?" she queried out loud.

What kind of parent would saddle a child with such a name?

One glance answered that question. Wearing brand-new jeans and looking up at her attentively was a miniature replica of Judson Horn—right down to blue eyes the color of a clear mountain stream.

"Is Cowboy your nickname?" she asked.

"No, ma'am," the child said, setting his jaw in the selfsame manner of his father. "It's real enough."

An errant whisper floated through the room. "Crazy fool greenhorn!"

Carrie spotted the culprit immediately. A beautiful child of dark hair and complexion, the boy's twin sister was surrounded by a tangible aura of anger.

The teacher's bright smile was lost on the girl. Sullenly turning her eyes to the top of her desk, Brandy refused to make eye contact. Reminded of the biblical passage about the sins of the father being passed on to his children, Carrie could tell this girl had a chip on her shoulder the size of the Grand Canyon.

Knowing the unflattering outburst was simply parroted from home, she tried not to hold the girl's surliness against her. There was no reason whatsoever that the school year had to stretch into an unproductive battle of wills. Besides, it wasn't hard to imagine the type of home life a man like Judson Horn would provide. The very names of his children suggested a conception that occurred when one mixed cowboys with brandy....

Curbing her highly inappropriate thoughts, Carrie directed the children to her name written upon the blackboard. Just as the empty grade book presented the small group assembled here with a fresh start, Carrie once again regarded her own life as a clean slate.

"Do any of you have any questions for me before we get to work?"

Immediately Brandy's hand shot up.

"Did you *really* set jackalope snares around the school?"

The room erupted into nervous snickers at the impertinence of the question.

So much for starting out without any preconceived notions, Carrie thought to herself.

"I most certainly did," she admitted with chagrin, countering yet another burst of tittering with complete candor. "As you know, I'm not from around here. So when someone pulled that trick on me, I fell for it. And even though it might seem funny to you, it hurt my feelings." She paused and looked directly at each one of them. "I'd like to ask you all a big favor."

This was a new turn of events. Every eye was on the lovely new schoolteacher.

"Since I'm new around here, I'm going to need your help to learn all about your beautiful state. I'd like very much for us each to learn from each other. I promise you that I won't ever pull such mean tricks on you. I won't allow anyone to be made fun of, say, for not reading as well as someone else, or maybe giving the wrong answer to a question. You don't have to be afraid of not knowing something here. I think school should be a safe and a fun place for you to come each day."

The children looked suspiciously at one another. Seemingly this sharing of the teaching task was a strange and exciting concept to them.

Cowboy broke the uncomfortable silence by raising two fingers in the air.

"Yes?"

Blushing furiously at the new teacher's ignorance, he explained, "I have to go to the bathroom."

"Oh," Carrie responded with a smile. "Then you have my permission to leave the room."

As he made his way around to the back of the building to get to the bathroom that had been added onto the old structure when indoor plumbing had become available, Cowboy stooped to open his pocket to let a water snake slither away in the long grass.

Despite the fact that it was a heck of a lot easier to simply let the kids catch the bus home, Judson deliberately arrived early that first day of school to pick up his children and check on the progress the new schoolteacher was making. He had no intention of any ill will between them affecting the way Ms. Raben treated his children.

"What the hell?" he muttered, rubbing his eyes in disbelief.

Decked out in their best back-to-school clothes, the entire group was sprawled out beneath a stand of aspens. In their midst was their teacher, looking cool as a southern breeze in a pink seersucker suit, her matching heels tucked neatly beneath her long, folded legs. Cheryl Sue used to wear expensive, out-of-place outfits just like that. Judson remembered how that pretty packaging had disguised the shallow, insecure girl inside. The one who preferred holding on to her daddy's money over the twins she had borne her half-breed husband.

Accepting a bunch of dandelions from a pupil, Carrie flashed the child a smile so genuine that even from a distance Judson could feel its warmth. Assuring himself that it was nothing more than sheer indignation that caused his heart to lurch so unnaturally against his chest, he wondered how school could have changed so drastically from the way he remembered it.

Parking his pickup at the edge of the playground, he proceeded to amble over to the assembled group.

"A little early for school to be out, isn't it?" he drawled.

"Daddy!" squealed Brandy, leaping up in delight, her artwork crumpled and forgotten in the grass. Adoration was clearly reflected in the girl's lovely features.

Looking up at Judson from ground level, Carrie had a positively erotic view of his tight jeans. Over the weekend she had begun to doubt whether this man was truly as mouthwateringly sexy as she had remembered him or if her imagination had merely run away with her. The immediate fluttering of her senses reassured Carrie that it was not her imagination.

Taking a deep breath she forced herself to address him coolly as "Mr. Horn." Still smarting from their last encounter, Carrie wished she could afford the luxury of ignoring him altogether. But since he was a patron of the district, not to mention the chairman of the duly elected school board, that would be impossible.

"I'm afraid you're mistaken. School is not yet out, and that means you're interrupting my class," she added pointedly.

"We're helping Miss Raben learn all about Wyoming," Cowboy volunteered. "See!"

Proudly he thrust his drawing at his father, whereupon the rest of the children held their creations up for his inspection, as well. There were drawings of lupines and dandelions and meadowlarks and aspen, and a remarkably fat bumblebee crayoned by a cherubic kindergartner.

Judson pushed his hat back in that damnable sensual

way of his and wiped the sweat away with the sleeve of his plaid Western shirt.

"Now ain't those pretty?" he said, rolling his syllables over in a slow, rough-hewn manner that gave a whole new nuance to the word "drawl."

"Aren't," corrected Cowboy, clearly embarrassed by his father's grammatical shortcomings.

Carrie bestowed upon the boy a smile so sweet as to cause his father's certain displeasure to fade into the distant horizon.

"Mr. Horn," Carrie said, firmly taking hold of the situation, "would you please remain after school for a moment?"

Judson bore the children's snickers humbly. Still, as he waited for them all to leave, fondly swatting his own two on the bottoms and telling them to wait for him in the truck, he felt his neck grow prickly at the thought of being held after school.

Positioning herself behind the fortress of her old oak desk, Carrie addressed him as she would any errant student. "I will not tolerate you undermining my authority," she began in a quiet yet commanding tone.

Judson met the cold anger reflected in those shamrock green eyes with the same defiance that had marked his own turbulent schooldays.

"How was I to know I was interrupting? What I walked into sure didn't look anything like school the way I remember it."

The remark only added fuel to the fire smoldering within the schoolteacher's eyes.

"I suppose not," Carrie countered in a tone that indicated she rather expected him to have been educated in a cave somewhere, possibly with a pack of wolves.

"Apparently," she continued without missing a beat, "it was not enough for you to humiliate me in front of the entire school board, you had to make certain that every child in the entire school district was informed of how I fell for that ridiculous jackalope story."

"Wait just a minute," Judson interrupted. "It's not fair for you to hold me entirely accountable for—"

Carrie did not give him the opportunity to finish.

"Evidently you feel I owe you an apology for being born in Chicago, for being born a woman, *and* for having the audacity to accept this job. Well, Mr. Horn..." She paused, letting him feel the full effect of her eyes as they bore into him like emerald drill bits. "Like it or not, I am here and I intend to stay!"

"I never said—"

"And despite your opinion to the contrary, teaching is damned hard work. I would greatly appreciate it if in the future you would refrain from undermining my authority. That means not bad-mouthing me in front of your children or any of my other students, thank you very much. As well as curtailing that 'you ain't never gonna need none of this here book-learnin' anyhows' illiterate attitude of yours!"

Judson visibly bristled. "Now wait just a damn—"

"All I'm asking you, Mr. Horn," Carrie interrupted, her voice rising to match her anger, "is that you get out of my way and let me teach!"

Pointing her red pen at him like a weapon, she dismissed him. "You may go now."

The silence that followed was deafening.

Judson was too stunned by the curt dismissal he had received and the tongue-lashing he had endured to know exactly what had hit him. The last time he'd felt like this was when a bull by the name of Hell's Belle had tossed him into the air like a tiddledywink, knocking the wind out of him.

Ears burning, he spun on the heels of his cowboy boots and slammed the door behind him, thinking wryly to himself that this was definitely more like school as he remembered it.

Judson Horn had spent his entire second grade at the back of the room, his desk turned away from the rest of the class because his teacher believed "Indians" didn't have the mental capacity to keep up with their white classmates. Left with a demeaning set of building blocks, he had been abandoned to his own devices. Angry, rebellious and innately clever, it was little wonder he turned his teacher's hair prematurely gray. Bitter memories of his alienated youth served to reinforce his determination that his own children be accorded the best education possible—despite any innate prejudices some damned Eastern transplant may harbor about their heritage.

And so it was with the same sense of rebellion that characterized his own difficult adolescence that Judson Horn turned his horse in the direction of the school—the very day after the new teacher's volatile warning to stay away. Though there were miles and miles of fences to inspect before bringing the summer herd down to winter pasture, it was the particular stretch bordering school property that Judson decided to check first. By God, nobody was going to keep him from becoming involved in his children's education.

Nobody.

Washakie, the big black stallion that Arthur Christianson had left to him, pranced high-handedly through the tall, yellowing grass. Thoughts of his father caused

Judson's chest to tighten as old conflicts blew across the open plains of his heart. How many times had he wished the man who had sired him had given him the thing he had desired most—his name.

Accepted as neither white nor native, Judson had plowed his way through a difficult childhood with both fists ready for action. His mother was of little help, allowing her son to shoulder the burden of his mixed parentage and her drinking problem as best he could. It wasn't that she hadn't loved her son; she'd simply wallowed her life away waiting for the man of her dreams to return, reclaim his family, and live happily ever after.

Judson had remained the old man's shameful secret well past his mother's death, unacknowledged until terminal illness compelled Arthur Christianson to make swift recourse with his past. A cruel smile curled Judson's lip at the thought of Harmony's founding father explaining to God from the depths of hell how leaving all his worldly goods to his blue-eyed half-breed bastard should, by all rights, procure his way into heaven.

Though Judson knew money couldn't buy the way to heaven, it had damn sure bought him a measure of polite respectability that had been absent in his life since the day his birth certificate had been stamped "father unknown." Judson not only inherited one of the finest ranches in the county but also dear old dad's seat on the school board. And while it was true that he had initially been appointed to his position upon Arthur Christianson's death, he had taken that responsibility so seriously that he had later been elected by his colleagues as chairman of the board. That the very first issue on which they had sided against him was the hiring of some wet-behind-the-ears, sassy Easterner certainly stuck in his craw.

Looking over a strand of sagging barbed wire, he caught a glimpse of Ms. Raben surrounded by a gaggle of happy children. It was near the close of the school-day, and they were hanging Popsicle-stick birdhouses from every low limb in the surrounding vicinity. Aspen leaves rustled softly like forgotten dreams, and a gentle breeze carried the sound of a woman's tinkling laughter.

Judson was keenly aware of the subtle changes taking place in the new schoolteacher. For one thing she had abandoned her fine dresses for jeans and tennis shoes. Observing the tight fit of demin over feminine curves, he felt the sudden stir of desire. It made it damned hard to remember just how much he disliked his children's teacher. In fact, the warm pressure pushing against his jeans was almost enough to make him forget the sting of a whip across his back.

Seeing the smile fade from Carrie's face the moment she spotted him, Judson felt the sharp prick of rejection. Clearly Ms. Raben hadn't softened any toward him. Well, how could he expect such a pretty, pampered Anglo princess to understand the forces that motivated him? Besides, he thought, swinging his long legs over the sagging barbed-wire fence, he didn't give a damn what she thought of him. Not a damn.

Certain that everything she did, including her choice of attire, fell well out of the range of "school as Judson Horn remembered it," Carrie wasn't particularly surprised when the man interrupted her lessons a second day in a row. Assuming that he would gleefully report back to the rest of the board scandalous accounts of her creative approach to education, she greeted his presence with cool indifference. On the outside, that is. On the inside, every molecule in her being was on fire. She found Judson's presence more than just a little unsettling.

On horseback, he looked the part of an old-fashioned Western hero. As he swung himself gracefully off the biggest horse she had ever seen and tethered it to the fence, Carrie reminded herself that she should be looking at him through the eyes of an employee, not a hot-blooded woman. One smooth move placed him on her side of the fence and in dangerous proximity. As he strode purposefully across the expanse of the playground, a devilish fist tightened around her heart.

What exactly was there about this man that caused her pulse to quicken so maddeningly? Her mother had warned her to stay away from such men. Men whose eyes could undress you and possess you in the selfsame glance. Men whose toughness in word and manner covered their feelings. Men whose rough hands conjured up unladylike images of silken bodies entwined. Men who could break your heart just as surely as they could break a wild mustang and abandon you the instant you were tamed—

"What lesson are we learning here today?" Judson asked the class in a most cavalier manner.

Carrie was in the midst of deciding whether she should make him the focal point of a lesson in social skills or simply answer truthfully that this was part of a science unit on birds when the sound of angry honking interrupted her.

A fat goose with a pink bow tied around its neck rushed out from beneath the steps of the old schoolhouse. Flapping its wings in consternation, the animal charged at Judson with malice in her yellow eyes.

The children exploded into gales of riotous laughter.

Raising a boot in self-defense, Judson looked at Carrie as warily as at the goose that held him at bay.

"Meet Mother," she said with the first genuine giggle he had heard from her lips.

The sound chased away the dark thunderclouds from his rugged features, and Judson crooked one eyebrow in her direction.

"Mother Goose?"

Nodding her head, Carrie smiled. "Your daughter had the honor of naming our watch goose."

"Your what?"

"I got to thinking about what you said—that I should buy a weapon to protect my students, but since I don't like the idea of guns being anywhere near children..."

"You bought a goose?" he finished for her.

Despite the fact that Judson was looking at her like she had temporarily misplaced her straitjacket, Carrie continued as if it were the most obvious solution in the world.

"Like I tell my students, when confronted with a problem the best place to look for answers is in the library. In my research I discovered that geese are mortal enemies of snakes, and I'm happy to report that since Mother has been on the job, she's killed at least two snakes that I know of."

Carrie simply could not resist adding with a self-satisfied smirk, "It appears she's just as adept at handling the two-legged variety, as well..."

Judson suffered the indignation of the remark by employing his trademark grin.

"And the pink bow?" he inquired. "Does research show that color causes less emotional stress to snakes?"

"No, it's just to make sure no trigger-happy hunter mistakes Mother for wild game."

Judson's smile deepened to reveal matching dimples at the corners of his mouth. His voice dropped to a huskier tone, and he tossed her a wink. "Here I was going to offer my services in teaching you how to use a gun and you've gone and eliminated the need."

That wink was Carrie's undoing. How could such an innocent gesture twist her insides into knots that would baffle the most experienced Girl Scout? A jab of disappointment sliced through her at the thought of losing an opportunity to let this incredible hunk wrap his arms around her again. If teaching her how to use a gun was anywhere as sensual as showing her how to set a snare, she'd gladly fire Mother and start packing a pistol.

Roughly Carrie reminded herself how truly astounding her reaction was. Had she forgotten that this man had made her the laughing stock of the county? A frown creased her brow.

"Honk! Honk!"

Mother apparently had picked up on Carrie's negative vibes. With wings outspread, the goose arched her slender neck and advanced upon her prey with the obvious intention of taking a series of well-aimed pecks at his leg.

Judson backed up a step. "Call her off!"

"What's good for the goose is good for the gander, eh, Mr. Horn?" Carrie smiled wickedly.

Now that the shoe was on the other foot, she was thoroughly enjoying herself. Dismissing her guardian with a slightly regal air, she reassured her, "You can run along now, Mother. I've got things under control here."

Mother hesitated.

It was galling to Carrie that even the goose seemed

to recognize the obvious lie—that she was far from being under control whenever Judson Horn was around.

"Go on," she shooed sternly.

Mother waddled off a little ways, and Judson cleared his throat. He looked at the faces of the children gathered around them, all expectantly watching him. For a man who could count on the fingers of one hand the number of times he had ever apologized, this was not going to be easy.

Sweeping his hat from his head, Judson assumed a contrite position. "I'd like to publicly set the record straight. It was wrong of me to lead you on the way I did about those jackalopes and..." He filled his lungs with a cleansing breath of fresh air. "I'm sorry."

The words came out in a rush. As his own children's mouths fell open, he silently dared them to say a single word.

Cowboy's face split into a wide grin. He sharply elbowed his sister, who seemed to be in shock.

Carrie knew exactly how Brandy was feeling. She hadn't thought it in this particular man's nature to admit to any personal wrongdoing. A public apology was more than she had ever expected. Clearly such an admission in front of his own children was not an easy thing for him. She scrutinized his face to ascertain his sincerity.

"I accept your apology, Mr. Horn."

Had he expected her to say anything else with her entire class looking on?

As a flicker of relief registered in those eyes of pure blue, the realization that this rough-and-ready cowboy had actually been nervous softened Carrie's heart. His vulnerability touched her.

The rest of the world faded away as green eyes

smiled into blue, and the animosity between them was replaced with a tentative feeling of friendship—and something more. Call it chemistry. Call it lust. Call it downright stupidity. Whatever it was, it crackled between them like electricity arching across a night sky.

And it was obvious to even the youngest in the group. Dismay illuminated Brandy's fine features as she moved to her father's side and possessively slipped her little hand into his.

The sound of a bus rattling down the dirt road reminded Carrie and Judson of where they were. Snuffy waved broadly in their direction as she brought the bus to halt in front of the schoolhouse.

"Class is dismissed," Carrie announced in a voice too shaky to convince Judson that she hadn't been affected by the moment.

She had stared into his eyes in hazy anticipation, and something inside him had gone completely still. Had the circumstances not been so damnably wrong, he surely would have covered those tempting lips with his own and sampled their promised sweetness. If only to get her out of my system once and for all, he lamely added as an afterthought.

"Come on, Daddy," Brandy entreated earnestly, pulling hard on his hand. "It's time to go."

Despite the warning lights flashing inside his head, he heard himself ask Carrie, "Will I see you at the Harvest Ball on Friday?"

The tiny pulse beating in Carrie's throat belied the emotions she was trying so desperately to fight. If she wasn't careful, she knew that small ache in her heart would explode into yearnings that she could not allow herself to feel. Yearnings that stubbornly refused to be ignored.

Despite her vow to keep her distance from any employer who made her so very aware of herself as a woman, Carrie found herself nodding her head in affirmation.

"I'll be there."

She had already received an invitation in the mail and had been informed that, as the newest member of this small community, her presence was expected in Atlantic City. Though reluctant to return to "Jackalope City," as she'd affectionately dubbed it, it was a perfect opportunity to get to know her students' parents in a social atmosphere.

What harm could possibly come from a simple community get-together? she asked herself, immediately blocking the frightening array of answers to that very question.

Judson's gaze was pinned directly on her, and Carrie's pulse bounded. So graceful and fluid was this man in the simple movements of everyday life, she couldn't help but wonder if he wouldn't prove to be a wonderful dancer, as well. Clearly Judson Horn was the type of man who would do everything to perfection—including making love…

Cursing herself for the blush that rose to her face, Carrie told herself that Judson's apology had set the tone for nothing more than a strictly professional relationship. She couldn't afford to blow that. She needed this job almost as much as she needed to believe she was in complete control of the romantic nature that she kept neatly tucked out of sight. Remembering how the past had so painfully enlightened her on the fact that romance was highly overrated, Carrie told herself she was far too old to believe in childish fairy tales. She may be going to a country-western ball, but she certainly didn't fancy herself as Cinderella.

And even though Judson Horn's incredible know-everything-tell-nothing blue eyes could melt icebergs, that didn't necessarily make him Prince Charming.

Chapter Five

Though Snuffy had told her that dress was informal, Carrie felt self-conscious in the Western clothing she had bought especially for the occasion. Cowboy boots clicking on hardwood floors, she felt like a fraud as she presented her invitation for the Harvest Ball at the historic Gold Diggers' Inn. It was accepted with a flourish by an older man in nautical garb who told her to "Just call me Captain." A woman with jet-black hair swept dramatically back from her face presented her with a room key. The proprietors, both New York City transplants, were deliciously eccentric. Feeling at home among misfits, Carrie felt suddenly glad that Snuffy had convinced her to splurge on an all-night "wingding." Renting a room for the night would save her from driving long, treacherous miles over mountain passes at night.

A familiar sound rose above the polite mingling of conversations in the room, vibrating deep inside her. Low and sexy, Judson Horn's voice alone was enough to raise her temperature to "simmering." As green eyes met blue across the crowded room, Carrie felt a band cinch tight around her chest, cutting off her air supply.

It should be illegal for a man to have eyes such a captivating shade of blue, Carrie thought to herself, keenly aware of the frisson of tension that made her skin tingle all over. In the few long strides it took him to cross the distance between them, she upbraided herself for her involuntary reaction, sternly reminded herself that their relationship was not of a romantic nature but rather one of rattlesnakes and bad practical jokes...and shared looks so devastating as to strip away her mask of cool indifference and leave her feeling naked in his presence.

Judson almost spilled his drink when Carrie entered the room. What had become of the stuffy Ms. Raben he had approached such a short time ago at the airport? Who was this sensual woman in tight-fitting black Wrangler jeans and a red silk blouse that clung to her like the subtle, suggestive fragrance of her perfume? Whoever she was, she made his head spin. As Judson noted that she turned every other head in the room, as well, a surge of sudden possessiveness jolted him. He was quick to note that he was the only Indian adrift in a sea of cowboy hats. The last time he'd stepped into an interracial relationship, it had almost cost him his life.

Purposely running a callused finger along the scar on his jaw, Judson reminded himself just how much trouble a pretty white woman could be. Unfortunately that reminder was of little use against the response that rose unwillingly deep inside his belly.

"Looking the way you do tonight, I'd say you should've brought Mother along to protect you."

His voice was as velvety as his gaze, caressing Carrie like a lover's experienced hand. In open appreciation he perused her at length, starting with her legs, hesitating at her breasts, and lingering thoughtfully on her mouth for what seemed a lifetime. In actuality it was but a few seconds, but in that brief length of time, it took an act of supreme self-control for Carrie to refrain from nibbling nervously at the pink lipstick she had so carefully applied earlier.

"I gave the dear old goose the night off," she replied more coolly than she thought possible.

Judson's unexpected compliment caused a burgeoning warmth to envelop her heart. Feeling her knees turn to the texture of warm rubber, Carrie sat upon an old-fashioned, red velvet settee. How could she possibly hope to retain any semblance of professionalism when he was looking at her like she was the main course for the evening?

Judson took a seat beside her, his nearness emphasizing the narrow span of the furniture and reminding Carrie of why it had traditionally been dubbed a love seat. In the process of making himself comfortable by stretching his long legs out in front of him, Judson accidentally brushed against her thigh. Even through layers of clothing the contact was searing. Carrie flinched as if she had been touched by a branding iron. Every brain cell screamed that she should jump up and run while there was still time to save herself.

"Jud!"

A breathy, feminine voice rang out like the crack of a rifle. And, like a shot, it found the center of the target imprinted squarely on Carrie's heart. A striking woman of Native American descent, wearing a filmy yellow dress and as much turquoise jewelry as her lean frame could support, swept gracefully across the room. Coming to a stop in front of the settee, she held a jeweled hand out to Judson and pulled him to his feet.

The smile that he gave her as he took her hand made something wrench painfully inside Carrie's chest. It was the kind of indulgent smile reserved for beautiful, accomplished playthings, not for modest, inexperienced types such as herself. Gruffly, Carrie reminded herself that she was not the type of woman who wanted to be valued solely for her outward beauty. A good mind, a clear conscience and a kind heart—those were the standards by which she preferred to be judged. Unfortunately such noble thoughts did little to fill the gnawing hole inside her.

"I'd like you to meet Carrie Raben," Judson said. "Carrie, Estelle Hanway, an old friend of mine."

Rising on unsteady legs, she reminded herself that it came as no surprise that Judson was involved with other women. Hadn't he, after all, made of point of telling her as much the first day they had met? And hadn't she herself already decided that nothing good could come of anything other than a professional relationship with the chairman of the school board? Just because lately he had thawed toward her didn't mean she should read anything more into it.

"So you're the new schoolmarm?" the dark beauty queried, arching a pencil-thin eyebrow in her direction.

Carrie grimaced at the antiquated term. "'Marm'? Why that makes me sound ancient!"

Estelle's big, brown eyes radiated hostility. A huge silver belt buckle cinched about her waist showed her trim figure off to its best advantage while attesting to

her status as a one-time rodeo queen. Carrie sensed in-
tuitively that this particular woman wouldn't hesitate to
rope any female competition like a calf at branding
time.

If she could have, she would have put Estelle's mind
at ease. If anything, the woman's obvious infatuation
with Judson only served to deepen Carrie's steadfast
resolve to keep things between them strictly professional. Her heart was still under repair—for the next
fifty or sixty years or so.

"Would ya mind gettin' me a drink, babe?" Estelle
asked, her voice as warm as dripping honey.

Noting with disgust how very like a puppy Judson
jumped to do her bidding, Carrie stiffened as the stat-
uesque woman eased herself into his vacant seat.

"Isn't that the best-lookin' rear you've ever seen on
a man?" she commented to his receding backside.

Carrie's only response was an awkward sputter.

"I see you've already noticed," Estelle commented
dryly.

Embarrassment stained Carrie's cheeks. This woman
so brazenly oozed sexuality that she felt drab and prudish by comparison. Discreetly dropping her gaze from
the topic of conversation, she was glad when they were
called to the dining room.

Throughout the first course, she tried not to focus on
how Estelle managed to eat everything on her plate with
one arm draped possessively over Judson's shoulder.
Swallowing hard, she forced herself to take another bite
of the delicious food set in front of her. She picked up
her glass of wine and took a gulp of the clear liquid.
Feeling a delicious warmth spread through her, she took
another sip. The pleasant, muzzy feeling slowly spread-

ing through her helped dull that sharp pain in her abdomen that she was loathe to recognize as jealousy.

"Did I ever tell you about the time I kicked Jud's fine-lookin' butt in a game of strip poker?" Estelle asked the people seated at their table.

Despite the fact that Judson vehemently protested, she refused to be quieted.

"And then there was the time in high school when Jud fastened a yellow bow tie on a fat, old sow, tied a banner to its tail with Principal Irmscher's name on it and staked it out in the middle of the football field. Oh, I suppose you being a teacher and all wouldn't find that particularly funny, but..."

On and on she regaled everyone with Judson's past exploits. Enjoying his discomfiture immensely, Carrie was delighted to see that he had no more control over Estelle Hanway than he did of the wind. His persistent attempts at shushing her were to no avail. As the anecdotes became wilder and more embarrassing for Judson, Carrie began to actually enjoy herself. Her laughter was contagious, and before long everyone was making a point of introducing themselves to the lovely, new schoolteacher who had so quickly won their children's hearts.

"No wonder Jake hasn't been complaining about his schoolwork this year," said one leathered patron. "Heck, if I'da had such a pretty, young thing as yourself for a teacher, I'da stayed in school a whole longer myself."

His wife good-naturedly rolled her eyes. "Hank's had a little too much to drink, but I do want to thank you for taking extra time with Jake. He's a little slow but he's a good boy. It was a daily battle last year just getting him on that school bus every day. I know you're the reason for his sudden change in attitude."

Another, stopping by to shake her hand, congratulated Carrie on bringing life back into an educational system too long dominated by "crochety old-timers."

Each one thanked her for her willingness to treat their child as an individual and expressed appreciation for her willingness to help any who lagged behind by extending her own work hours. Eager to welcome her into the community, most made a point of mentioning their approval to the local board members in their midst. Their warm handshakes and heartfelt praise filled her with the first genuine sense of belonging since the day she'd blown into Wyoming on that fateful, dusty wind.

Anxious to work off some of the calories they had just consumed, everyone was eager to follow up dessert with dancing. While famous for its cuisine, the Gold Diggers' Inn was not equipped with a dance floor, so a band was awaiting them next door at the mercantile. Though she had little desire to watch Estelle fawn all over Judson on the dance floor, Carrie could find no gracious way to excuse herself from the festivities. She certainly didn't want to seem uppity to these people who had so graciously invited her into their tight-woven circle.

The pocked face of the moon illuminated the boardwalk for the sated group that threaded their way toward the bar where a country band by the name of Prairie Heat awaited the young-at-heart. Stopping on a narrow bridge to admire the brook that looped the old ghost town like a silver ribbon, Carrie lingered to drink in the silent beauty of the night. The gentle babbling of the creek was a welcome respite from dinner's loud and

often bawdy conversation. Dazzled by the stars overhead, she could scarcely believe that she was so very
far removed from the hustle and bustle of the big city.
In her silent revery it almost seemed as if she had truly
stepped back to a more innocent time in history. A time
when women allowed men to open doors for them without worrying that anyone would consider them weak,
when falling in love didn't automatically mean falling
into bed, and when an engagement ring meant your fidelity was pledged to another for life....

Seeing her bathed in moonlight, Judson stopped up
short. Cold and perfect in her beauty, Carrie appeared
to him a marble statue. All night long he had been as
unable to take his eyes off of her as he was to shake
off Estelle's suffocating nearness. For the life of him,
Judson couldn't figure out why he wasn't attracted to
Estelle the way she wanted him to be. The way *he*
wanted to be. It would be such an easy remedy to the
sexual dearth in his life—an occasional roll in the hay
with a beautiful woman whose skin color and expectations were like his own, at least on the surface. Behind
Estelle's easygoing attitude toward sex, Judson suspected she nurtured the hope that once lured into her
bed, he would someday marry her. And that just wasn't
going to happen. With anyone.

His life was devoted to his children. Well aware of
the teasing they had endured because of his "half-breed
ways" and unusual appointment to the school board,
Judson wasn't about to subject them to the lewd con-
jectures of neighbors and classmates regarding their
daddy's love life. He remembered how it felt to defend
his own mother's honor on the playground day after
day. How painful it had been for him to watch her stum-

ble drunkenly from one man to another in the vain hope of erasing Arthur Christianson from her heart. How hurtful to have it thrown in his face by his schoolmates.

Not the kind of man who would settle for what he could get rather than what he really wanted, he wouldn't repeat his mother's mistakes. And what he wanted, Judson reminded himself, was freedom, complete and inviolate.

No matter how often he told Estelle that nothing more could come of their relationship than friendship, he seemed unable to convince her of that irrefutable fact. After his disastrous, short-lived marriage, he had never again been tempted to give his heart to another.

Snatches of the past flashed through his mind: a secret elopement, the bright lights of Reno, a week of sheer heaven and a descent into hell. Their marriage certificate meant nothing to Cheryl's brothers who'd proceeded to lay him open with a whip as if he were nothing more than a side of beef. And though they never laid a hand on their sister, they broke her spirit just the same that fateful day. Nine months later, McLeashe sold his ranch and moved his family back East. Back where respectable white girls who had fallen astray were decorously wrapped in high society and allowed to maintain that the mistakes of the past never happened.

"There's no place for these breeds where we're going," read the note attached to the twin bundles Judson found upon his doorstep one crisp, bud-tight spring morning. The first time those babies looked into his eyes they captured his heart. Cradling them gently in his arms as he sat on the steps, he vowed that day to provide them with the kind of safe, carefree childhood of which he himself had been deprived.

Standing in the moonlight contemplating Carrie's

lithe silhouette, Judson would have liked nothing better than to have been left alone with his thoughts. But Estelle, yanking hard on his arm, pulled him toward the country music blaring through the ancient, swinging doors of the mercantile.

Stepping into the smoky bar, it seemed to Carrie that the jackalope on the wall was actually smirking at her. *So who needs you to tell me I'm an idiot?* That fact was already assured by the way her heart lodged in her throat as she watched Estelle drag Judson onto the dance floor. It was impossible not to notice what a truly striking couple they made, both so natural and at ease in their movements.

Luckily, Carrie was given little time to brood. How she became the center of attention was beyond her, but it seemed as if suddenly every unattached man in the room was lined up to ask her to dance. It occurred to her that these tongue-tied, stoic Western men used dancing as a means of expression. Letting the lyrics and the rhythm of a song speak for them, they danced as wildly and as eloquently as the music allowed.

By the time the last strains of "Mommas Don't Let Your Babies Grow Up To Be Cowboys" had faded, a bevy of eligible, young fellows was gallantly offering to teach her how to swing dance. A particularly gregarious bronc rider by the name of Cody Trent finally succeeded in coaxing her to her feet. With a victorious smile, he placed his black felt cowboy hat upon her head.

Judson, who had been watching Carrie move from one dance partner to the next, gritted his teeth at the intimacy of Cody's gesture. *God, but she's a beautiful woman.* Something utterly sensual in the swish of her light brown hair held him a distant captive. He noticed every minute detail about her: how her smile lit up the room, how Cody's hat framed her heart-shaped face, how his hand rested suggestively on the small of her back....

Openly scowling at them from the bar, he devoured Carrie with his dark, smoldering gaze. As Cody led her toward the dance floor and into a lively two-step, jealousy and anger sprouted a split vine inside Judson's battered heart.

As keenly aware of the sawdust beneath her feet as of Cody's hand placed snugly on the small of her back, Carrie considered exactly what it was about cowboys that held such worldwide allure. Perhaps in this time of confusion as to whether a man should be a warrior or a poet, both sexes were drawn to the clearly defined image of the cowboy swaggering in the certainty of his own masculine identity.

As Cody swung her gracefully along beside him, Carrie laughed aloud with the sheer exuberance of just being alive. Bestowing a dazzling smile upon her partner, she solemnly vowed to kick up her heels more often.

When the band switched to a slower melody, Carrie slipped from Cody's arms. Turning to seek out her chair, she ran smack-dab into Judson's broad chest.

"Would you do me the honor of this dance?" he asked, sweeping the hat from his head. The seductive timber of his voice shifted Carrie's pulse into double time. She had never met a more appealingly dangerous man in her life.

Letting his gaze linger on her flushed countenance before falling to the full, soft swell of her breasts, Judson's eyes narrowed with predatory interest.

"I promise to go real slow."

That silken promise brought carnal images to mind, and Carrie forced the air into her lungs in short, shallow gulps. Where was that iron will she had always before been able to exercise over such wayward thoughts? The challenge glistening in the depths of those cerulean blue eyes left her helplessly entranced. The God's honest truth of the matter was that Carrie had been wondering for quite some time what it would be like to dance a slow one with Judson Horn.

Against her better judgment, she nodded her head yes.

A magical something passed between them as he took her hand in his and led her to the center of the crowded dance floor.

This is dangerous. Dangerous and exciting... Carrie thought to herself, hoping that she wouldn't trip over her own two feet and again verify his opinion of her as a bumbling Eastern dudette.

Those thoughts fled the instant Judson wrapped his arms around her and pressed her close against his chest. Assailed by his clean, masculine scent, she felt the heat shimmer over her skin as she was lifted away by the intensity of emotion that washed over her.

"You're very beautiful," he said, succumbing to the temptation to brush aside a stray lock of hair from her eyes. Judson felt its silky texture between his fingers. A kitten could be no softer.

Carrie's only response was an inaudible sigh. That wonderful heat coming from his body made her feel warm all over. As she nestled her head against his shoulder, she felt him tighten his hold around her waist. For one fleeting moment, she put aside her fears and allowed herself the indulgence of floating away to the strains of a romantic waltz enfolded in a pair of arms that she suspected could be just as gentle as they were strong.

Next to hers, his heart beat savagely, stirring her own blood to its wild refrain. Carrie told herself that what she was feeling was insane. Aside from the insurmountable fact that he was her boss, Judson Horn was totally wrong for her. They had absolutely nothing in common. Any fool could see that a relationship with such a man was destined for failure. She was pretty sure he held more affection for his livestock than he ever could for a woman! Still, whatever she had once upon a time felt for Scott was nothing compared to the bombardment of senses and emotions that Judson evoked in her. This was like being swept away without a raft in a raging river. This was going over a waterfall and rejoicing in the certain destruction that lay at its end. Crashing, crashing, crashing into the mists of passion....

With a start Carrie realized that the music had stopped and that she and Judson were center stage, lost in one another's arms. Feeling the scrutiny of the whole assemblage, she stepped out of the circle of his warm embrace.

With flushed cheeks, she hurried back to her table.

Estelle was waiting for her.

"Jud's one helluva dance, ain't he?" she asked, her dark eyes narrow slits.

Carrie took a long swallow from the glass of punch Cody had given her. Never before had a drink tasted quite so good.

Feeling her way as cautiously as if she were walking through a minefield, she answered, "He certainly is."

For the first time all evening, Estelle chose her words carefully. "Did you know that he and I used to win dance contests all over the state when we were just kids?''

Carrie shook her head no. "It wouldn't surprise me."

"Even way back then I had my cap set for him. Did you also know he broke my heart by eloping with the prom queen the same day we graduated high school?''

Carrie's eyes darkened as she tried to picture Judson as a young man in love.

"Of course..." Estelle added, taking a sip of beer and looking at her as though from behind the sights of a rifle. "The little white princess's brothers were none too happy about her marrying a breed."

"Enough!" Judson's voice was a low growl.

"What're ya afraid of?" queried Estelle, meeting the icy fury in Judson's eyes head-on. "That once our lily-white schoolteacher knows you're a half-breed she'll expect you to begin every sentence with 'how'?''

Crackling with anger, her laughter rose hyenalike into the dark, smoky air.

"You never did have sense enough to stop when you were ahead, did you, Stella?" Judson's voice was the sound of dry reeds rustling in the wind as he turned and walked away.

Fondling her beer bottle, Estelle turned her ire upon Carrie. "Don't think I haven't noticed the way Jud looks at you," she snarled. "I'm afraid he's done gone and gotten himself twitterpated over you, city girl. It's for your own good that you know just exactly what you're letting yourself in for."

"Surely you don't think—"

Continuing as smoothly as if Carrie had not even opened her mouth, Estelle wasn't about to let herself be interrupted. "I don't hold no grudges against you *personally*—it's just your kind is all."

"My kind?" Carrie asked, dumbfounded.

"The white kind. The wrong kind for Jud."

Tearing at the label of her beer bottle with long, red fingernails, Estelle laid her heart on the table. "I don't mind admitting that I'm head over heels in love with Judson. It ain't no secret. Everybody knows it. But to be honest with you, short of hog-tying him, I don't think there's any way to ever get him to make that trip to the altar again—and definitely not with another white gal. Whether or not he's willing to shack up with one is another matter, though I dare say the parents 'round here might take exception to that kind of an arrangement—you being a role model for their precious little darlings and Jud being chairman of the board and all... Not to mention how well an interracial affair would be received amongst the *good folk* here."

Estelle's crude remark was another pointed reminder of how fragile Carrie's status in this community really was. She had an ugly premonition that this conversation was on the verge of erupting into a free-for-all. Still curious despite her intense desire not to be, Carrie remained rooted to her seat. It was hard to refrain from asking all the questions rushing through her mind. What difference had race played in Judson's first marriage? How had his brothers-in-law entered into the picture? And how could anyone as stunning as this woman fail to capture any man's heart she set out to claim?

"Well, don't say you ain't been warned. Just remember a breed's an outcast, accepted by neither Indian nor white," Estelle said, throwing back her head and downing the last of her beer. "And the scars you can see ain't nothing compared to those you can't."

Setting the empty bottle down on the table with a hollow thud, she stumbled to her feet, adding shrilly,

"Oh, and one more thing... When you get a chance, tell that son of the devil he can find himself another baby-sitter for those ornery twins of his!"

With a swish of her yellow skirt and a jangle of turquoise jewelry, Estelle passed through the swinging doors of the Atlantic City Mercantile and into the black Wyoming night.

Stepping up beside Jud at the bar, Bill Madden ventured a question. "So what do you think of our new teacher now?"

"She'll do, I guess," was Judson's terse response.

Still smarting from his confrontation with Estelle, he was inclined to think all women were more trouble than they were worth. It would probably be wise to just call it an early night.

"I knew if you'd just withhold judgment until she'd had a chance to prove herself, you'd—"

"And I'm telling you to wait and see what happens when winter hits full-blast and life-of-the-party *Ms*. Raben discovers subzero weather is more than what she'd bargained for. When, come midterm, our kids are left without a schoolteacher and there's damned little chance of finding a replacement!"

"You're too young to be such a curmudgeon," the superintendent said, slapping Judson on the back with a familiarity that, considering his present state of mind, was a tad risky.

"She's terrific! The kids all adore her, and every parent I've talked to purely gushes with praise for her."

Judson wasn't listening. He was looking thunderously at the table where Carrie sat as the belle of the ball. By the way she had reacted when she thought he was drinking a beer on the ride from Rock Springs, he'd assumed that she was a teetotaler like himself. He'd also paid attention at dinner, noticing that she had stopped at one glass of wine. He remembered her telling the waiter that she seldom drank, and unless he'd been mistaken she hadn't been drinking anything else but punch the rest of the evening.

So that dazed look on her face just didn't add up—not until Judson caught sight of a silver flask from under Cody Trent's jacket. Suddenly it was as plain as that stupid jackalope on the wall that he was spiking the punch. The way he kept pouring it down Carrie between dances made Judson wonder how the poor thing was able to stand at all. It was obvious to him that a certain stud was intent on taking advantage of their pretty new schoolteacher.

Catching a glimpse of bewilderment glistening in eyes the color of a spring meadow, Judson felt a hot gush of protectiveness well up inside him. Damn it all to hell! When had he gone and gotten so soft in the heart? What difference was it to him whether this little greenhorn was in over her head or not?

Judson didn't take time to consider the answer to those questions. Pushing back his hat, he wondered how in hell he was ever going to pluck this innocent, little lamb from the midst of a pack of wolves without getting himself killed in the process.

Snuffy and her husband were off jitterbugging with gusto, leaving Carrie surrounded by men vying for her attention. For the life of her, she couldn't understand why she was suddenly feeling so giddy. Her head was spinning as she smiled demurely at the blur of faces around her.

"I don't remember any of my teachers looking like

you," simpered Ted Barrows, a young man destined to inherit one of the most successful ranches in the county.

Pulling up a chair, Judson ignored the hostile glares he received from the other men as he edged in beside Carrie. Leaning close to her, he whispered in her ear, "I think you've had enough for one night. Why don't you let me walk you back to your room?"

At the sight of Judson's arm draped about the object of his desire, Cody Trent bristled. "Excuse me, but Carrie and I was just about to scoot a boot on the dance floor."

Judson pushed his Stetson casually back to better reveal eyes the color of gunmetal. "Why don't you just scoot your butt out the door instead?"

Cody jumped to his feet. "And why don't you just try to make me, *chief*?"

Standing, Carrie placed herself precariously between the two men. Her head was swimming.

"Maybe you're right, Jud," she interjected woozily.

"Sit down," commanded Cody, never taking his eyes off Judson for a second. "I ain't about to be shot out of the saddle tonight, leastwise not by a damned breed!"

The room grew ominously silent. The band trailed off in midsong as every eye in the bar swung to the two men facing off center stage like bull elk locking horns.

"You already have been, cowboy," Judson countered smoothly. "Next time, why don't you try hitting on a lady without lacing her drinks first?"

Slipping an arm protectively around Carrie's waist, Judson turned and directed her toward the door. She screamed a second too late to warn him of Cody's wild roundhouse swing. The blow caught Judson square in the eye. He stumbled, dropping his arm from around

Carrie, who landed with a squeal upon a hard chair of knotty pine that skidded across the floor before coming to a halt and dumping her unceremoniously on the floor.

"Come on," Jud muttered, righting himself and blocking a flurry of frontal jabs.

There was something frightening in Jud's eyes as he took on his adversary. Something latent, primordial and savage lashing out at all the injustice in the world with the force of a piston. All the pent-up hurt and anger deep inside him went into a solid uppercut that connected with Cody's nose with a sickening crunch. Blood spurted as the shorter cowboy fell to his knees clutching his nose.

"Ya broke it, ya sonufabitch!" he cried, watching the blood flow through his fingers in bright red gushes.

A couple of Cody's friends rushed forward to grab him under each arm. As they dragged him ignominiously out the swinging doors, the cowboy mumbled through thick lips, "Don't think I'll forget this, ya stinkin' Injun dog."

Carrie's knees were weak. The echo of that threat beat against her head like the steady thumping of war drums. She fought the urge to scream hysterically when she covered her face with her hands and discovered they were splattered with bright flecks of blood.

"Oh, my God," she groaned.

"He'll be okay. I've had my nose broken lots of times," Judson reassured her, trying to downplay the incident.

Carrie looked at him in amazement much the way he assumed Jane must have first looked at Tarzan.

"Come on, let's get out of here," he said, wiping a streak of blood from his face and directing her outside into the crisp autumn air.

"Are you all right?" she questioned, the concern in her voice as caressing as the cool night breeze that enveloped them.

"I'm fine," he replied gruffly. "How about you?"

Because she was not really sure, Carrie declined to answer. She could make out the tracks in the dirt where Cody had been hauled to the safety of a waiting vehicle. "Do you think he'll carry through on his threat?"

"Don't know," Judson said slowly, looking into the depths of those misty sea-green eyes as if searching for something that had eluded him all his life. "It's never smart to make an enemy if you can help it, though I've made plenty of 'em for a hell of a lot less."

Carrie wondered if "a lot less" entailed having had the misfortune of being born neither completely brown nor white in a world that set such great store by the color of a person's skin.

"It's all my fault," she murmured by way of apology.

Brushing aside the hair that fell across his forehead, Carrie gently inspected his eye. Already it was swelling into an ugly purple mass. As her fingertip brushed against his cheekbone, she felt Judson quiver beneath her touch. Her fingers trailed the white ridge of the scar along his jawline and reluctantly dropped to her side. So much pain was written in that rugged, battered face. She wondered if Estelle was right. Could any woman ever tame his wild, skittish heart?

Beneath her heavy thoughts, Carrie felt herself sway. She was grateful for the steady support that Judson offered. As he guided her slowly down the old boardwalk in the moonlight, she drank in every detail of the man beside her: the mingled scents of cologne, smoke, sweat and blood; the determined set of his jaw; the raw power emanating from every pore in his body. And though Carrie was appalled by the fight she had just witnessed, in some dark cavern in her heart, she had secretly thrilled to it. She felt protected and cherished.

The porch light back at the inn illuminated Judson's bloodstained shirt as he opened the front door to let Carrie enter. It only took him a moment to discern that she was in no shape to navigate the way to her room by herself. Though the fresh air had helped to clear her head, Carrie was nevertheless unable to walk down the middle of the narrow hallway without bouncing off the walls.

"I feel awful funny," she admitted with a hiccup.

"I imagine you'll probably feel worse in the morning."

Suddenly Carrie felt herself being swept up into a pair of masculine arms. Wrapping her arms around the strong column of his neck, she nuzzled against him, shamelessly enjoying the sheer strength of this man who had so savagely defended her honor.

"Judson?" Running her hands along the width of his shoulders, she looked him straight in the eye.

"What?" The single word was but a rasping chord stuck in his throat.

"Are you twitterpated?" The question sent Carrie into a fit of tinkling laughter.

He wasn't amused. "Which room is yours?" Judson asked from between clenched teeth.

"Search me," she giggled.

As her laughter faded to a soft, enticing sigh, Judson felt the fire of desire licking in his loins. She certainly wasn't making this easy for him. Such an adorable morsel would be easy pickin's for any randy cowboy on the make. He thanked God that he had been able to get her away from the bar. He seriously doubted whether Cody Trent would have exercised the same restraint.

"Where are your keys?" he demanded in an angry whisper.

"I told you, search me," she whispered seductively.

Something akin to summer lightning flashed in Judson's eyes. He set her down and pressed her back against the wall. Unbuttoning the pearl fastening of her blouse pocket, he slipped his hand inside. Beneath the cool, red silk, Judson felt how warm and very soft her breast was, and he stifled a groan as the nipple hardened under his caress. Sliding his hands down the length of her, he stopped momentarily to encircle the small circumference of her waist before plunging his hands into both back pants' pockets. He noted that Carrie's shapely behind was as firm and rounded as he had imagined. He pulled her toward him, grinding his hips into her, making sure she felt how hard she made him. He was rewarded with a slight gasp. Continuing on, one front pocket at a time, Judson delved their depths stopping just short of the inviting warmth between her legs.

"Damn," he muttered out of frustration and need. "I still can't find the key."

Carrie smiled coyly, her eyes heavily lidded. "That's because I didn't lock it. It's room number seven."

Lucky number seven, Judson thought to himself. Lifting her cotton-candy lightness back into his arms, he carried her to her room. With one hand, he turned the knob and pushed the door open with a boot.

"Will you tuck me in?" she asked, her eyes heavy-lidded.

"Do you have any idea what you're doing to me?" Judson asked thickly.

But it was too late.

Carrie's eyes were closed, and she was already breathing deeply.

"Damn you," Judson murmured, laying her as gently atop the bed as a bouquet of wildflowers. "Don't you dare pass out on me!"

There was no response from the still body sprawled invitingly upon the lacy patchwork quilt. Judson lingered over the sight of her light brown hair splayed across her pillow and fought the urge to explore every inch of those soft, womanly curves. But despite what Cheryl Sue's brothers had wanted to believe, he was not the type of man to take advantage of a woman—no matter how tempting the situation.

Raw need strained from every pore in Judson's body as he pulled off Carrie's tight, squeaky-new boots and made himself stop where his imagination refused to. Tucking the covers around her, he wrapped her cozily from neck to toe, a picture of perfect innocence.

"Poison. Pure sweet poison…" he muttered in a strangled voice as he headed for the door.

Chapter Six

Waking was agony. Carrie opened her eyes to sunlight streaming through yellowed lace curtains. Fighting her way out of a haze, she drew her arm out from under the covers to check her watch. It was almost noon, she was in a strange bed, and she had no idea how she had gotten there. Like a fish rising to the surface of a murky pool, flashes of recollection glimmered just out of sight: snatches of a conversation with Estelle Hanway, a bloody brawl, the apparent consumption of alcohol she didn't even remember drinking....

"Great first impression on the parents of the community..." she moaned into her pillow, envisioning Carry Nation and her dedicated disciples of Christian Temperance descending upon her little schoolhouse with her hatchet, a sack of feathers and a bucket of hot tar.

A note fluttering on the pillow next to her caught her attention. Flinging back the covers, she sat straight up. A wave of nausea washed over her as a mountain of fireworks exploded inside her head. Clutching her aching head between her hands, she made herself focus on the note.

Will be moving cattle for the next couple of days but count on seeing me at Open House this Thursday. We'll continue the search for that missing key then...

Jud

The sight of that masculine scrawl caused Carrie's heart to beat out a deafening staccato. Pulling the covers up over her head, she tried to block an onslaught of perplexing questions. Just what did that reference to a "key" mean? How could she face the parents of the community at Open House knowing what a complete and utter fool she'd made of herself last night? And how could she possibly confront Judson again when her memory was fuzzy at best?

A knot of emptiness tightened in an already-sour stomach. Though Carrie didn't remember spending the night with Judson, his note definitely placed him in her room. If he chose to leave her hanging like dirty laundry flapping in the breeze, she could well imagine how a conservative community that held its teachers to a strict display of moral standards would react.

Gingerly climbing out of bed to face herself in the mirror, she asked her reflection, "Carrie, what have you done?"

Disheveled and red-eyed, her image regarded her gravely.

Crumpling the note in her hand, she cursed, "Damn your blue eyes, Judson Horn!"

* * *

The following day found Carrie crouched in front of the old potbellied stove, rubbing her hands together in disbelief. The cold weather defied the calendar. Why just yesterday she'd needed only a sweater to keep warm. Apparently Judson hadn't been kidding when he'd warned her of blizzards as early as September. Without so much as a whisper of protest, the glorious fires of early autumn had been obliterated overnight. A soft, persistent snow fell as gently as if from her grandmother's worn flour sifter. Looking at her own delicate fingers, Carrie thought of her grandmother's hands: the knuckles enlarged, the skin splotchy, a lifetime of love and hard work etched upon them. If only Granny could somehow pass on to her the ancient strength in those gnarled, veined hands!

She was sure Granny would make short order of this old potbellied stove—and of any man as aggravating as Judson Horn for that matter. Try as she might, Carrie had been unable to banish intrusive thoughts of the man whose cryptic note had left her hanging by her fingernails.

She crumpled sheets of old newspaper and stuffed them into the maw of the stove. Then she neatly stacked several thick logs atop, lit the paper and waited for the warmth to begin thawing out the chilly room.

Flames leapt like bright orange tigers...and died just as quickly. Frowning, she sacrificed more newspaper to the ill-natured stove and lit it again.

"All right, you sorry son of a Ben Franklin, fire up!" she commanded.

Grinning behind its open grate, the crotchety stove remained indifferent to her pleas.

What she needed to build a proper fire, Carrie belatedly realized, was some kindling. Determined not to be

beaten by an antiquated piece of iron, she marched back
to the woodpile intent on splitting at least enough to last
her through the week.

When he spotted Carrie awkwardly wielding an ax,
Judson felt an odd catch in his chest. She almost toppled
over backwards beneath the weight of the heavy tool
hoisted high over her head. He started to get out of his
pickup to offer his assistance, but the look of sheer determination upon that lovely, soot-streaked face stopped
him in his tracks. Abe Lincoln she obviously wasn't,
but there was a look in her eyes that caused him to
wonder if she might not be distantly related to Lizzie
Borden!

Clearly this woman had something to prove to that
old woodpile, and he dared not interfere.

What exactly was it, he wondered, about this woman
decked out in an old coat and sweatpants, swinging an
ax, that he found so inexplicably endearing? Dressed
thus, she was far more appealing to him than the fash-
ion-conscious Easterner who not so very long ago had
stepped off the plane at Rock Springs.

Plucky Ms. Raben was proving full of surprises. Judson had to admit that he had been wrong about her from
the start. Far from shying away from her responsibilities
as he had predicted, she instead embraced them whole-
heartedly. Judson knew that the fact Carrie was an outsider had merely provided him a convenient excuse to
distrust her. Past experience provided the foundation for
his suspicions. His ex-wife had spent the better part of
her high school years trying to convince him that racial
prejudice was merely an outdated phase in American
history well on its way to virtual eradication by an enlightened press. Ironically, she'd failed to win her own

family over to that belief, and it was surely a merciful God who had prevented Judson from being beaten to death in their brotherly act of retribution for his crime of loving a white woman.

The labored sound of chopping called Judson back to the present. It was beyond all reasoning that the sight of his children's teacher was able to stir in him something so urgent that it threatened to overshadow the bitter lessons of the past.

Don't be a fool! he told himself fiercely and, pressing the accelerator to the floor, left without making his presence known.

Jud was running scared, and he knew it.

The rest of Carrie's week passed in a blur. Open House was scheduled Thursday evening to accommodate working parents who couldn't get off during the day. It was held the second week of school just so parents and teachers could get acquainted with one another without getting too hung up on grades so early in the year. Carrie just managed to squeeze in dinner before parents began a steady parade through the doors of the old schoolhouse. Far from the dismal turnout which school functions warranted at her old school, all the parents and guardians turned up. Every parent save one.

Carrie could only surmise by Judson's noticeable absence all week and the fact that Cowboy and Brandy had been riding the bus to and from home that their father was either still moving cattle as his note had indicated or that he no longer felt the need to check up on her. As twilight succumbed to night, she found herself wondering if Judson would make his promised appearance at all. She had just about given up on him when she caught the far-off purr of an engine.

Seconds later a gleaming black snowmobile shrieked to a halt just outside her door. A picture of the devil himself, Judson took off his helmet, tucked it beneath his arm and made his way up the front steps with a cheerful whistle on his lips.

How he managed to look sexy sporting a big black eye was beyond Carrie, but that was exactly the term that came to mind when he sauntered out of the dusk and into the light of her classroom. Dressed in tight jeans and a faded denim shirt, he looked every inch a country road warrior. His only concession to the cool outside temperature was a worn leather jacket and a pair of sturdy gloves.

Feeling a wave of heat go through her, Carrie wiped her sweaty hands on her skirt. Was God's only purpose in making such heart-stopping men simply to test women's fortitude? As he stood there holding his helmet in his hands awaiting his turn to speak with her, Carrie had a vision of him in his youth. She felt a sudden pity for his mother as she thought both of Judson's broken noses and of his shattered marriage. The poor woman's life surely was a succession of administering to one black eye after another.

Thinking how Cowboy was bound to be the spitting image of his father, Carrie felt a vise tighten around her heart. She prayed that the hooded pain in Judson's eyes would never dim the ever-present sparkle in Cowboy's cornflower blue ones. There was something so utterly captivating in the boy's happy-go-lucky attitude that Carrie lost all objectivity where he was concerned.

Funny—while she'd been so busy protecting her heart from Judson's charms, both of his children had rushed in and stolen it outright.

Carrie tried to focus her attention on Mr. and Mrs.

Benson, who were on their way out the door. While Tommy's father was a taciturn man who seemed to observe her from behind a mask of wrinkled leather, Mrs. Benson was effusive in her praise.

"Tommy's never been much for school, ma'am, but since you've showed up, he's excited about learning. I can't get over the change in him," the woman said, bubbling over with enthusiasm. "We can't thank you enough for offering to tutor him after school."

Mr. Benson shook Carrie's hand, expressing with a firm squeeze the appreciation he was unable to put into words. She felt a rush of gratitude to all of the genuine folks who had gone out of their way to make her feel truly accepted into their close-knit community. As the door closed behind the Bensons, Carrie's eyes glistened with emotion.

Snow was steadily piling up in huge, fluffy marshmallow mounds outside the window. As Judson skirted the rows of desks in a few, long pantherlike strides, it seemed to Carrie as if a twist of fate had somehow left them the only two people alive on earth. That sexy, loose cowboy gait sent her heart somersaulting as suddenly he was wonderfully, frighteningly close. The faint smell of bottled musk mingled with his own unique masculine scent in an intoxicating combination that sent a curling sensation spreading through her like warm honey.

Wincing at the sight of a garish black-and-blue eye, she murmured apologetically, "I am so sorry about that."

Feeling as guilty as if it had been her own fist that had delivered the blow, she reached up on tiptoes to inspect the nasty plum-colored bruise. It proved almost impossible to dismiss the overwhelming urge to kiss it better.

"It's nothing," he replied with an indifferent shrug.

Instantly aroused by Carrie's feathery touch upon his swollen cheek, Judson wondered if, like a chosen few of his people, she was blessed with the gift of healing. Where her fingers touched, his skin tingled, and a swift stab of desire, hot and urgent, surged through him. His mind fought against the truth that his body was so eager to embrace. Had he ever wanted a woman quite so badly?

He tried to move. Couldn't.

Self-control was a thin wall holding back his need to devour her, body and soul. The flame of his desire was mirrored in Carrie's eyes. Looking into those hungry eyes, Judson decided, was like being held in the vortex of a tornado. And caught in the eye of that tornado, the rest of the world spun out of control. Minute details sprang into vivid clarity: the clean scent of shampoo tangled in hair highlighted with gold and umber; thick eyelashes shading a pair of kelly-green eyes unguarded and trusting; the sensuous curve of red lips open in breathless expectation.

The invitation was unmistakable.

Judson had never wanted anything more in his life than to claim the sweetness of those lips.

He was going to kiss her! Carrie thought, tottering beneath the realization that she desperately wanted him to. Unfortunately his attempt to steady her by placing both hands on her shoulders had quite the opposite effect. Her bones turned to the consistency of melted candle wax.

All that stood between them was the tiny sigh that escaped her lips. The pounding of her heart echoed so loudly in her own ears that she couldn't help but wonder if Judson could hear it, as well.

Peering into the depths of those sky-blue eyes, Carrie watched a battle being waged. Pain creased Judson's brow with the effort, and his hands knotted into fists at his sides. Witnessing lust succumb to restraint in the grapple, Carrie realized that she was wrong about that kiss after all.

Damn! When was the last time she had been right about a man? Scott was a liar, but she had trusted him right up until the moment she had been confronted with the undeniable truth. On the other hand, Judson had told her up front that he didn't much care for her; she had refused to accept that. Perhaps she had only imagined the raw desire smoldering in the depths of those blue eyes.

It certainly wouldn't be the first time she had deluded herself. Though Carrie had believed Scott respected her decision to save herself for marriage, he later alleged her prudish ways had pushed him into the arms of that eager, young nymphette. The memory of those senior girls making sport about her virginity was still excruciating. She suspected their mocking laughter would ring in her ears forever.

What was it about her that men found so utterly resistible?

Deliberately busying herself with a stack of papers, Carrie attempted to turn the conversation to the topic of his children.

"Cowboy is a delight to have in class."

"He likes you."

"I like him, too."

A tender note leaked into her voice. The boy had somehow managed to work his way into the most secret part of her heart. Since the first day of school, the charming, little imp had proven an intractable ally, showering her with everything from apples and artwork and an amazing array of "critters" for science class. And although the thought would surely provoke his father, Carrie secretly hoped to cultivate the child's innate love of learning and broaden his horizons beyond the corral that housed his prized horse.

"And Brandy?"

"She's extremely bright."

Hearing the reserve in her voice, Judson pressed for the rest of the story. "But?"

Forcing herself to separate her feelings for the man from his children, Carrie briefly considered withholding her personal opinion. Needing to be sensitive as well as honest, tact was called for when discussing any child, let alone the chairman of the school board's feisty little moppet. Still Judson had every right to know her concerns about his daughter's social development, and, whether he liked what she had to say or not, he *needed* to hear it.

"But some days she's so angry that she verges on being unteachable. She has no trouble mastering the work, but there's an impenetrable wall around her that makes it almost impossible to reach her."

A perceptive glint illuminated those eyes of bluest blue. Having had some disturbing glimpses of his daughter as a soon-to-be rebellious teenager, Judson welcomed Carrie's opinion. Little did she know just how much influence she already exerted in his daughter's life. Like his son, Brandy was fond of quoting her teacher on a daily basis, and since Carrie had taken over the class, Judson had noticed a definite softening around the edges of his rough-and-ready tomboy.

"Suppose she gets that from me," he said, adding with a philosophical sigh, "She'll come around sooner or later, I figure. I'm afraid I'm not much of a mother to her..."

The admission prompted the questions rattling inside Carrie's head to tumble out without regard to consequences. "What about their mother? Do you share custody?"

Like a shadow playing across the face of a mountain, raw emotion crossed Judson's features.

"As far as my children are concerned, their mother is dead."

"Surely you don't mean that! What would make you say such—"

Though he had every intention of telling her to mind her own damned business, the harsh truth instead exploded from Judson's mouth. "Because I haven't heard from her since she dropped them on my doorstep and turned her back on us all forever."

He hadn't meant to disclose anything so personal. It was a pair of eyes the exact color of newly budded aspen leaves that was at fault, he decided. Something gentle and reassuring glimmered in their depths, inviting complete trust. How he longed to share with another human being the heavy burden he had been carrying alone for so very long, but his stubborn pride and cultural upbringing didn't allow for such weakness.

It would be too hard to keep the emotion from his voice to admit that the quarter of his native blood coursing through his children's veins was what had prevented them from being accepted into the haughty McLeashe family. That fair European line deemed the offspring of their daughter's ill-fated match to be nothing more than an appalling blunder to be remedied as quickly as pos-

sible. Even as smitten as Cheryl Sue had been with him
at the time, she had not been willing to risk complete
disinheritance.

Choking back the bile that rose in his throat, Judson
reminded himself of how grateful he was to her nonetheless. It would have been far easier for a frightened
eighteen-year-old to have gotten rid of her babies than
fly in the face of her family's wrath and carry the seed
of his love to term. That in an act of desperation she
handed the twins over to him was the greatest gift she
could ever have given him.

When his own life had seemed most hopeless, they
had provided him a miracle—a reason to go on. Those
two bundles of needy, squirming infancy had kept him
from falling into the same bottomless bottle of whiskey
that had claimed his once-beautiful mother.

Last he'd heard, Cheryl Sue had married a well-to-
do lawyer in Boston. Rumor was she hadn't been able
to give him any children. Maybe it was, as some said,
God's justice, but Judson doubted it. Personally he
didn't perceive God as being that spiteful and small.

Somewhere in the back of his mind a nagging worry
pricked at his consciousness. Just the thought of Cheryl
Sue someday trying to lay claim to Brandy and Cowboy
closed the hand of fear around his heart.

I'll bring down the entire McLeashe clan first!

Carrie wondered if it were possible to freeze in the
blue ice of Judson's eyes. She could not fathom how
any mother could just up and walk away from her children. It was, in her estimation, an unnatural act of ultimate betrayal. No wonder Judson's saddlebag was so
filled with cockleburs. It also explained why Cowboy
was so starved for motherly attention and why Brandy

insulated herself against the rest of the world, women in particular. Glad that she had worked so persistently and patiently with the recalcitrant child, Carrie's heart filled with empathy. If anyone was in need of a friend she could trust, clearly it was Brandy Horn.

Carrie regretted that her curiosity had resurrected such painful memories. Yet now that it was out in the open, for Brandy's sake Carrie knew she had to pursue her gut instinct.

"I'm concerned about your daughter. She's critical of others to the point of being rude. She's hostile when called on in class, and she picks on the boys at recess."

Judson's guffaw at her last remark failed to derail Carrie's train of thought.

"I suspect that beneath that tough cowgirl mask is a frightened little girl who could use some professional help."

Judson stiffened. His own dealings with modern psychiatry had left him openly wary. Time and time again hadn't the people from Family Services said they were only doing what was best for him? And time and again hadn't they proven themselves liars?

He had been the same age as the twins when his mother died of liver failure, leaving him completely on his own. Recalling the well-intentioned efforts of the "professionals" who placed a scared little boy into one foster home after another, Judson felt his stomach tighten. It hadn't taken him long to realize that many foster parents were just in it for the supplemental income generated by their charity.

When he spoke again, his stiff tone matched his posture. "Brandy doesn't need any damned psychiatrist examining her head. She's just going through a phase, and that's all there is to it."

"I don't think so," Carrie responded evenly.

"It's not that I don't appreciate your deep concern," Judson drawled with affected politeness, "but Brandy's my daughter, and I'll deal with her as I see fit. I don't want any snoopy shrink poking at her with a bunch of nosy questions—or you, either, for that matter."

As silence filled the space between them, Carrie's eyes shimmered with unspilled tears. "Of course, you're entitled to your privacy."

The professional tone she assumed didn't quite manage to hide the hurt in her voice. Had Judson slapped her, he couldn't have hurt her more deeply. Not only didn't he value her professional judgment, he flat out didn't want her butting into his life. Despite the fact that Brandy's pain was so obvious, Carrie knew that she had to respect Judson's wishes. As he had so pointedly reminded her, he was the girl's father.

But that didn't mean she had to agree with him. Or give up hope. After all, persistence was one of her strong suits.

Seeing the open resistance reflected in Judson's countenance, Carrie decided to pursue the matter at a later time. She closed her grade book, signaling that the conference was at an end.

Judson wasn't about to be so easily dismissed.

"Not so fast."

A masculine finger beneath her chin tipped her face up, and Carrie found herself lost in the spinning universe of Judson's blue eyes. The ice in those eyes had been replaced with a twinkle of devilment.

"There's still the matter of a missing key to discuss."

Praying that sanity would return if she could only manage to ignore that maddening swirl of heat low in her stomach, Carrie fumbled for a response.

"I don't know what you're talking about."

"Let me guess," Judson murmured in a voice tinged with reproach. "You don't remember teasing me into a full body search for a nonexistent key, right?"

The slow, soft tone of his voice was velvet against her skin. Carrie shivered as a flicker of recollection sputtered to life. Suddenly she remembered only too well how she had practically thrown herself at him! Scott had once taunted her with hateful words like "frigid" and "prude." Judson had every reason to employ their antonyms. If he hadn't thought her suitable to teach his children before, what must he think now? Two bright coins of color stained her cheeks pink.

It was obvious from the stricken look on Carrie's pretty face that she thought he had taken advantage of her. And that hurt. More than it should have. Somehow Judson had let himself believe that Carrie was different than the rest, who were so eager to believe the worst about the savage red man. Angrily, he told himself that she deserved to be kept dangling from his teeth like a mouse hanging by its tail, but somehow he wasn't up to playing any more games. He'd deliberately misled her once before, and all that had gotten him was one implacable, guilty conscience.

"Let me put your mind at ease," he said, and the flat tone of his voice hinted of a fatigue born of time and experience. "Nothing happened that night."

"Nothing?" Carrie repeated dumbly. What she remembered of Judson tucking her into bed hadn't seemed like nothing to her.

Hurt that he'd had so little trouble in brushing aside her sexual overtures, Carrie tried hard to sound grateful. "Thank you for being such a gentleman," she said stiffly.

Her gratitude filled Judson with chagrin. He knew he didn't deserve it. What would she think if she knew how difficult leaving her that night had really been? Familiar with lust, Jud feared that what he was feeling was more than that and it rendered him virtually helpless. Foreboding seeped into his bones like the cold Wyoming winter. Having been burned once before, Judson had promised himself never again to let any woman exercise that kind of power over him.

Just being near Carrie was too damned dangerous for his own good. And for hers. He was in desperate need of something to sweep away the deceptive fog invading his senses. There was only one issue left for him to address before his conscience would allow him to take off and leave sweet temptation behind for good.

"You're not expecting anyone else, are ya?"

Noting that the only vehicle parked outside the schoolhouse was his snowmobile, Carrie shook her head.

"Then this is the perfect opportunity to let me introduce you to your winter transportation."

Caught completely off guard, Carrie stammered, "W-what? Tonight? Are you crazy?"

Her thoughts fled to the massive snowmobile to which he referred. She hadn't so much as peeked underneath the heavy tarp that covered it and, in all honesty, had little desire to ever familiarize herself with it.

"Some people think so," he readily admitted, taking a single key from the rack behind her. He dangled it enticingly in front of her.

"But there's nothing like a moonlit ride on a snowmobile to clear the mind. Besides, you do need to know how to ride it, and I promised our superintendent that

I'd personally see to it that you know how to operate our emergency winter equipment."

Judson attacked Carrie's hesitancy with a boyish grin. "That is, unless, of course, you're chicken...."

Those childish words sounded like an indictment against all fainthearted womanhood. How could such a juvenile challenge stir her blood? Carrie wondered, even as her mouth was forming the words "You're on!"

Chapter Seven

An early model snowmobile lay sleeping beneath an aged tarpaulin. As Judson removed the snowy cover, Carrie surveyed the machine critically. It was bigger and far more formidable-looking than she remembered. Glad that the dark of night covered her face, she sucked in her breath, vowing not to let Jud see just how nervous she was.

"I'll start it for you," he said, throwing a leg over deftly.

Carrie leapt back at its firing up as if she had been shot. "It's loud," she yelled over the deafening roar. Black smoke rolled from the exhaust pipe. "And smelly," she added.

"Ready?"

Carrie hesitated. All around her heavy snow was falling. Tilting her face up, she caught a perfect crystal upon her tongue. When she looked again at Judson, it was to view him through a snowflake caught on the end of her eyelashes. Bedecked in prisms of light, he looked heaven-sent. Surrealistically surrounded by a pocket of warmth and contentment, Carrie wished there were some way to halt time.

The bitter cold was sure to follow the fantasy of this crystal fairyland.

Carrie had changed from her professional clothes into a one-piece snowsuit that should have been the furthest thing from seductive. The slick material hugged and highlighted her womanly curves, and Jud's attention was riveted to a zipper that ran the length of that incredible body.

Get hold of yourself, he told himself sternly. The last time he'd mistaken a bad case of runaway hormones for love had almost cost him his life.

Reluctantly Carrie took the ominous black helmet that Judson offered her and put it on. Climbing atop the snowmobile, she slipped her arms around Judson and braced herself against the onslaught of emotions that ran through her as their bodies made contact.

"This is the throttle," he said, pointing. "And this is the brake."

The snowmobile eased forward. Carrie tightened her mittened grip around Judson's waist. She closed her eyes, and only when her stomach settled did she open them. There was something comforting in pressing up against Judson's back as a fine, powdery snow sprayed up from the runners on either side of her. The ride was far smoother than she had anticipated, the snow obliterating any trace of the rocky road to Harmony.

As they turned sideways, the runners dug in. Snow shot up in a rainbow arc as Judson brought the machine to a sudden stop. Carrie was reluctant to release her hold. It had been a long, long time since she had allowed herself to cling to anyone.

Climbing off the machine to stand beside it, Judson urged softly, "Now it's your turn."

Carrie stiffened. A coyote's baleful howl echoed in the distance, sending a shiver along her spine. The snowmobile's power seemed as tangible as the frosty air filling her lungs. Well aware that learning how to drive this machine was a necessity, she scooted forward on the seat to assume the driver's position, and resigned herself with an audible sigh.

Judson hopped on behind, and Carrie felt her temperature rise. What was there about this man's touch, even through layers of clothing and in the midst of falling snow, that set her body afire?

"Where to?" she called over her shoulder.

"Wherever you want."

She gave the snowmobile a little gas, and they jerked forward into the wilderness dark. Bit by bit, Carrie became braver. Slowly she increased the pressure of her thumb upon the throttle. Faster they sped through a tree-lined path. It was exhilarating to feel the pull of the runners through the fresh snow. It was as intoxicating as the man holding on to her.

Downy flakes against the black night created a surrealistic sense of timelessness. Carrie was seized by the magic of sheer, unrestrained power. Like nothing she had ever felt before, riding through the snow was like breaking the sound barrier or blasting into another dimension. Speeding forward into an open field, she turned the machine up a whitewashed hillside and zoomed to the summit. The lights of a distant city glimmered sixty miles away, making her feel simultaneously insignificant and omnipotent. Feeling Judson's grip tighten around her, she wondered if he, too, felt the same sense of awe.

Making a wide arch against the slope, Carrie began the steep descent downhill. Disregarding the brakes, she raced downward, savoring the sensation of floating inches above the freshly fallen snow. The laughter bubbling in her throat froze upon her lips as a small ditch appeared immediately in front of them and they were suddenly airborne.

Thrown as if from the back of a bucking bronco, Judson landed in a snowdrift up to his waist. Carrie came down upon the back end of the runaway snowmobile with a thump. She grabbed for the brake as the machine careered out of control, but it was too late. The snowmobile sideswiped an aspen, bending it back like a twig. Tipping on the left runner, the machine flipped onto its side and pinned Carrie beneath its entire weight.

She was not hurt, merely crushed deep in soft layers of snow. Once her heart stopped pounding so raggedly, she felt panic succumb to utter despair.

Lying on her back and staring up into the black sky and the falling snow, she felt the tears slip down her cheeks. In the short length of time that it took Judson to sprint to the overturned machine, her mind filled with self-recrimination. He had been right all along. Clearly she was not the right person for this job. If she couldn't manage a snowmobile with assistance, how in the world would she manage a snowbound emergency in which a child's life might be at stake? Why had she ever left the relative safety of the city? What had ever led her to think that she could run away from the pain of the past? Her heart overflowed with bitter tears.

Judson's heart was beating so wildly that he feared his chest might just split wide open. A delicate woman was trapped beneath five hundred pounds of machinery, and he was responsible for it. He covered the distance to the overturned snowmobile in five seconds flat. Adrenaline surging through his veins, he flipped the heavy snowmobile over as if it were a toy. Kneeling beside Carrie's inert form, he removed the helmet from her head.

His voice was an off-key echo in the crystalline night. "Are you all right?"

"I'm fine!" she sputtered, bracing herself for an angry scolding about the lethal combination of city slickers and speed. Her tears shimmered in the moonlight.

Judson longed to kiss them away. Instead he pulled her to his chest and held her tight, as if he would never let go.

"Thank God," he murmured, brushing the hair from her face. It was at that moment he knew he had to have her—no matter how dangerous the consequences. She looked utterly devastated, and breathtakingly beautiful. Recognizing the agony in those unguarded eyes, Judson realized that she carried the same nameless emptiness inside as he. Was it possible that they could fill that void in one another?

Doubling up her fists, Carrie beat them against the flat plane of his broad chest. "I hate you!" she screamed into the vortex of the night.

And at that moment she truly did hate Judson Horn. She hated him for making her take a moonlit drive on this monstrous contraption, for seeing her so frightened and vulnerable, for his stupid practical jokes, for his hasty assessment that she wasn't good enough to teach his children, for the way he made her feel guilty for the sins of her white ancestors, for his past loves, for blurring that line she had so clearly drawn between her professional and personal life.

But most of all she hated him for making her want him as she had never wanted a man before.

Though her blows pelted him like bitter hail, Judson did not loosen his hold. Quietly the snow continued to fall around them, enveloping Carrie's tears in soft cotton.

He held her without saying a word until, at long last, her rage spent, she fell limp in his arms.

"I hate you," she whispered the last time before becoming forever lost in a blizzard of emotions.

"No, you don't," Judson replied, cradling her head in his hands and slowly closing his mouth over hers.

It was a kiss as light as the falling snow. The sky and the stars and the snowflakes swirled madly around them. The hard strength of Judson's body and the unexpected softness of his lips vanquished Carrie's resistance as quickly as a snowflake melts against warm flesh. She clung to him as though he were the only point of stability in a world spinning off its axis.

His kiss deepened as he probed the secret pleasures of her mouth. Carrie shuddered. But not from the cold. *Fire and ice,* she thought to herself. Judson Horn was both. His kisses more passionate than she had ever imagined, she responded without thought to the future. Carrie writhed with pleasure in his arms. From behind dark clouds, a golden band of moonlight stretched upon the bed of snow. Squeezing her eyes shut, Carrie lost herself in a storm far beyond her control. Nothing made sense anymore.

She hated Judson Horn.

And she loved him.

No logical pattern of common sense could convince

her foolish heart otherwise. Carrie had fought against it
so long that she dared not whisper the truth lest, as
Estelle had assured her, it would send him scurrying in
the opposite direction like a frightened jackrabbit.

With a groan, Judson pulled away. Her eyes wide and
brighter than the moon shining overhead, her hair a
shimmering halo about her face, Judson thought Carrie
truly a snow angel. There was, however, nothing angelic
about him, he thought ruefully. He knew that if he
didn't stop kissing her this very instant, he would succumb to his own hard need and take her right now in
this blanket of snow. It took all of his restraint to fight
his own hot desire.

"You scared the hell out of me," he growled, knowing that what really frightened him was the thought that
if this woman ever realized the power she wielded over
him, he would be rendered as helpless as a baby. He
had believed that his disastrous marriage had left his
heart impervious to feminine attention. Now he wasn't
at all sure that was true.

Carrie's hysterical outburst had shaken Judson to the
core. In a very short time he had come to characterize
her as tenacious and strong. There was an aura of gen-
tleness about her that reminded him of a most delicate
but deceivingly hardy wildflower. The thought that such
a lovely blossom could so easily be crushed turned his
blood to ice.

The concern reflected in Judson's face assured Carrie
that he did truly care for her—perhaps more than he
was ready to admit. That realization caused hope to leap
to life in her bosom like the sparks of a fire opal.

"We'd better go," Judson said huskily, pulling her

to her feet. "It wouldn't do for the teacher to be out with pneumonia, now would it?"

Even the very way that he brushed the snow from her body was infinitely sensual. Carrie felt herself sway, and though she was grateful for his steadying arm, what she really wanted was to dizzily succumb to more of his kisses, to let him take her this very instant and show her how splendid loving a man could be.

As Judson inspected the snowmobile, Carrie meekly inquired, "How bad is it?"

Bad, he thought to himself. *Worse than anything I ever imagined.* But since she was not asking about the state of his heart, he replied, "Just a nasty scratch on the side. If anything more serious is wrong, it'll show up on the way back."

Despite the dangerous consequences of that possibility, the thought of being stranded in the middle of nowhere with Judson was far more appealing than Carrie dared admit aloud.

"I'm sorry..." she began.

"No need to be," he replied, plucking both helmets from the snow and shaking them clean. "The only way to learn is by doing, and sometimes that means making mistakes. The important thing is to learn from those mistakes. It was good to see you gun it like that. You can't be afraid of a machine, but you've got to learn that it doesn't make you invincible, either."

"I meant I'm sorry about hitting you," she clarified.

Judson's eyes were warm spots in the cold landscape.

"I don't mind being used as your punching bag. Believe me, it's better to get it all out than to keep it inside and let it eat you alive."

Surely he was speaking from experience. True to his words, Carrie did feel purged. The cold and the pain and the blows and the kisses had somehow helped to cauterize that hurting part of her that ached whenever she remembered her ex-fiancé's betrayal.

Having had quite enough of driving for one night, Carrie slid behind Judson as he pointed the snowmobile in the direction of home.

"I don't really hate you," she said as a guilty afterthought, but her words were lost in the roar of the engine.

The ride home was slow and controlled and though it was not long, by the time they pulled up in front of her trailer, Carrie was shivering.

"I brought you a present," Judson said, walking her to the door.

"A p-p-present?" Carrie's teeth chattered.

"Go get into something warm, and I'll bring it around."

She was perplexed. What could it be? she wondered, watching Judson make a path through the snow to his pickup. Quickly she slipped out of her wet clothes and into a pair of jeans and a sweater.

By the time she returned to the front door, Judson was parked directly outside. He rolled down the window and yelled, "Where do you want it?"

What she discovered when she looked into the bed of his truck evoked a smile so warm it threatened to melt the newly fallen snow. Much better than traditional gifts of roses or perfume, Jud's present was a pickup load of kindling!

Chapter Eight

In the week since Open House, Brandy's sullenness had deepened into outright animosity. Yesterday the simple request that she rewrite an illegible assignment had brought on a temper tantrum that had earned the girl ten minutes in time out. The day before she had been reprimanded for pushing in line. The day before that for saying a bad word.

The confrontation which had been building had the feel of an old-time shoot-out at high noon.

"You're not my mother, and you can't tell me what to do!"

Arms akimbo, Brandy challenged her teacher in front of the entire class. Standing defiantly rigid beside her desk, she refused to erase the message she had written on the chalkboard when Carrie's back was turned.

"Go home Jackalope Marm!"

Carrie took a deep breath and checked her watch. "The rest of the class is dismissed for recess."

Taking her time arranging papers on her desk, she

waited for the last student to leave the room before meeting Brandy's icy sapphire eyes straight-on.

"What's this all about?" she demanded.

"Why don't you just go home where you belong?" the girl snapped.

"What on earth would make you say that?"

Carrie truly wanted to understand the reason for Brandy's sudden public display of antipathy. In the three weeks that school had been underway, she had made a determined effort to reach out with kindness to the youngster who bristled like a porcupine whenever she was offered a simple compliment. No matter how surly or contrary Brandy reacted, Carrie persisted in chipping away at her defenses with patience and kindness. And up until Open House, she had felt certain that they were making progress toward establishing a positive connection. Had Judson repeated her concerns and somehow upset the girl?

"You just should, that's all," the child mumbled.

"Come on, out with it," Carrie persisted. "You can be honest with me."

At this, Brandy quirked an eyebrow exactly as her father did before speaking his mind. "Okay—you don't have to leave, but I want you to leave my daddy alone!"

The earnestness of the entreaty rendered Carrie speechless. Aware that Brandy was closely monitoring her reaction, baiting her for any defensive response that would help justify her blatant disrespect, she knew it was crucial to remain not only calm but also empathetic. Carrie chose to let Brandy have her uninterrupted say.

Tossing a long, dark braid over her shoulder, the girl offered a curious explanation. "You're no good for him... You're gonna get him in trouble!"

Carrie's brow wrinkled in confusion. Since when did

Judson Horn need protection from anything or anybody?

"What kind of trouble are you talking about?" she asked.

"The kind of trouble an Indian gets into when he looks at a white woman the wrong way! The kind that'll get me killed on the playground!"

Carrie was shocked. Recalling Cody Trent's barroom racial slurs, she realized she really shouldn't be. In a community as small and conservative as this, it was little wonder that Brandy had been privy to some unsavory stories about her father's background. What she didn't realize was that Judson himself had openly discussed the scars upon his back with both his children. That a couple of Brandy's classmates continued to embellish the story just to see her fly into a rage was common knowledge to everyone but Carrie herself.

A profusion of questions tumbled through her mind. Had she somehow been the cause of someone taunting Brandy or Cowboy at recess? Had Judson perhaps broached the topic of their budding relationship with his children? Was the chemistry between them as obvious to everyone as it apparently was to Brandy? Could her feelings for him really put him in danger?

Seeing the girl's hands clenched into tight fists at her sides, Carrie worried more for any would-be tormenter than for Brandy herself. A formidable opponent for even the older boys in the class, Brandy would likely make short order of any woman casting sidelong glances in her father's direction.

Suddenly the cause of the child's misbehavior seemed obvious to Carrie. Having been the queen of the house for over a decade, Brandy wasn't about to give up her position without a fight. Frightened by the pros-

pect of losing her most precious possession—her father—she had come up swinging.

"You're just like her!" Brandy stormed with a mewl
of pain.

Carrie understood that she was referring to her
mother, the woman Judson said had abandoned the
twins at birth.

The vulnerability so carefully hidden behind Brandy's hard tomboy facade rose to the surface as tears
puddled in eyes so very like her father's. Though Carrie
longed to reach out, wrap her arms around the child and
quash all of her fears, she didn't dare. The probability
was high that the girl would react like a cornered wol-
verine. Suspecting that the girl carried inside her the
deep-seated belief that she was unlovable and had
somehow caused her mother to reject her, Carrie felt
certain that Brandy needed time, patience and a good
counselor. The hard part was going to be convincing
Judson.

Taking the girl's hand into her own, Carrie squeezed
reassuringly. That Brandy did not immediately pull
away was encouraging.

"Don't you think maybe you're overreacting? You
have nothing to fear from me, Brandy," Carrie continued gently. "Love isn't a competition. It's never lessened in the giving."

Carrie knew it might be too much to expect a child,
so deeply hurt and scared, to reason like an adult. Already having lost her mother, Brandy obviously
couldn't afford risking the loss of her father, as well.
But Carrie persisted, trying to reason with her.

"Sweetheart, don't you know how much your father
loves you? That nobody in this whole world can take
him away from you?"

Crossing her fingers behind her back, Brandy asked with false nonchalance, "Do *you* know that Daddy's going to marry Estelle?"

The news struck Carrie like a meteor. White-hot pain sliced through her. Exposed to this unexpected revelation, all the lies she ever had told herself about not falling for Judson simply fell apart.

Anger immediately followed on the heels of anguish. Carrie resisted the urge to grab the closest object and fling it against the wall in a temper tantrum to rival the eruption of Mount St. Helen's. She was an idiot, and all men were jerks out to play her for the fool. Judson Horn and Scott Ballson were the same under the skin— brother skunks.

It was hard to believe that a man could kiss her so passionately without giving any indication that he was actually engaged to someone else. Carrie couldn't imagine when it could have happened. Then again, Estelle had made quite a point of telling her that Judson wasn't the marrying kind, and as mad as she had been the night of the party, the fiery beauty had left Carrie with the definite impression that their relationship was on the skids.

Was it possible that Brandy had simply made the whole story up for reasons of her own?

Politely congratulating Brandy on her father's upcoming wedding, Carrie sent her out for the last few minutes of recess. Bright and early tomorrow morning she intended to pay Mr. Horn a visit at home. If Brandy was lying, it would simply highlight the need for her to seek counseling. If she was telling the truth, Carrie would simply have to make Judson rue the day he'd ever been born.

* * *

Judson prided himself on the fact that there was little on earth that scared him. And that's what made Carrie's kisses all the more disturbing. They left him shaking in his size twelve boots. Something in those feathery-soft kisses resurrected a demon he thought he had slain a long, long time ago. For the past two nights, his sleep had been riddled with erotic, impossible dreams that left him sheathed in sweat.

Even if he could bring himself to simply stay away from Carrie in the future, which he sincerely doubted, she would probably suspect the truth—that he was avoiding her out of pure fear. Fear that history would repeat itself in the same ugly pattern etched upon his back. This time, however, Judson knew there was more to consider than just himself. He had to think about how any relationship he entered into would ultimately affect his children. His first obligation was to them. And though he had the sneaking suspicion that Cowboy would be delighted to see his father's relationship with his teacher blossom into something more constant, he wasn't sure how Brandy would react.

Shucking off his covers, Judson decided that it was a perfect day to ride out to check on his hunting camp before the season opened—anything to put as much distance between him and the enchanting pair of emerald eyes that had tormented him throughout the nights.

Besides it was a matter of necessity to get things ready for the arrival of the rich Eastern clients whom he was expecting. What they were paying for was a trophy hunt, not any part of the work required to make it happen. It would certainly be easier to make preparations now while the weather was still relatively nice than to try and fight the snow and bitter cold that was sure to come.

* * *

Carrie was up with the sunrise Saturday morning determined to seek out the truth of Brandy's claim that her father was soon to be married. She poured herself a cup of coffee to drink on the way over to Judson's ranch, the Blue Sky Lodge. Though much of the snow from earlier in the week had already disappeared, it felt like the cold had settled in for what was going to be a very long winter. Patches of thin ice cracked beneath her boots as she made her way from her pickup to the corral where Judson was in the process of saddling up his favorite stallion, a black cutting horse, Cowboy had told her was named Washakie.

The uneven ground, stamped by tire treads and horse hooves, was muddy in spots where the ice had yielded to the sun. Carrie had dressed appropriately in jeans, a bulky coat and boots. She stopped for a moment to observe Judson pull himself into the saddle with the unconscious grace of a natural athlete. Tall and at ease in the saddle, Carrie thought the expression "larger than life" fit Judson Horn as well as those worn jeans that caused her pulse to flutter so. When he finally turned his head and marked her presence, she noticed that the contours of his face were as sharp and clean as the Wind River Mountains looming in the background.

His sexy Western drawl was slow and easy. "What brings you here so early on a Saturday morning?" he asked, characteristically getting to the point without any small talk.

The gravel in that voice was unmistakable in the way it wound itself around her nerve endings. The memory of this man's kisses was still warm upon her lips, sending a quiver of liquid fire to a place low and deep in her body. The sky was as vivid blue as the eyes that swept over her.

In that instant Judson noted that Carrie had on the same shiny, new boots that she had worn at the Harvest Ball and a pair of jeans that caused a man to consider the need for a cold shower.

"I need to talk to you."

Her tone indicated that this was not a social visit, and the sudden surge of joy Judson felt at seeing Carrie so unexpectedly was replaced by an ominous sense of misgiving.

It had been his experience that whenever someone from school came calling, it meant trouble. Many had been the time when he had covered his mother's drunken form beneath a blanket to face the authorities by himself, armed only with the standard line that his mom was too sick to come to the door.

Carrie's somber manner created a sense of déjà vu that made Judson instinctively protective of his own brood. What had those two rascals of his been up to now?

Beneath the brim of his hat, blue eyes issued a challenge as he bent to offer her a hand. "Hop on if you want to talk. I've got business to attend to."

Carrie eyed the beast critically.

A cynical smile curled Judson's lips. He was sure she had about as much desire to spend time on horseback as he did attending a high society tea.

But Carrie had only to think of her reason for being here to put aside her apprehension about climbing atop a horse as big as a building. She firmly clasped Judson's outstretched hand. He pulled her up with little effort, leaving her to figure out some way to keep from falling off the back end of the horse.

Judson kneed the horse, and Carrie was pitched forward against a back as sturdy as the wall that she was certain to encounter in the ensuing conversation. Slipping her hands around his waist, she made a wild grab for the saddle horn.

"It's not a brake," Judson chided, covering her hands with his own.

How rough those hands felt against her own smooth skin. Unbidden images of those masculine hands caressing every inch of her body caused Carrie to squirm uncomfortably. Each surefooted step the horse took along the trail jostled her against Judson's lean, hard body. Feeling her heart beating rhythmically next to his, she became aware how very like two nesting spoons their bodies fit together.

Amazed at how truly powerful the animal underneath her was, Carrie could better understand how a man like Judson was so intrinsically connected to the land. The horse himself seemed an inviolate link to his independent way of life.

After a while Judson asked, "What's so pressing that you felt the need to make a personal house call?"

"I understand that congratulations are in order."

"What for?" Judson asked, thinking perhaps one of the children had won some kind of an academic contest.

"On your upcoming marriage to Estelle Hanway."

Judson pulled hard on Washakie's reins and twisted around in the saddle to look her square in the face. "Where in the hell did you get that idea?" he demanded in an accusatory manner.

"Brandy told me."

"Where'd *she* get that idea?"

"That's what I'm here to find out," Carrie replied evenly.

"Well, it certainly wasn't from me!"

Seeing the doubt and the pain reflected in the endless meadows of Carrie's green eyes, Judson found himself on the defensive. Every time Estelle brought up the issue of matrimony, he had made it perfectly clear that he wasn't ever going to marry again. He doubted that she was the source of this disquieting rumor.

The whole thing was as puzzling to him as the wariness reflected in Carrie's manner. True, he had deceived her with that harmless jackalope story, but after the way he had kissed her the other night, Judson couldn't imagine that she would doubt his feelings toward her. What kind of a man did she think he was anyway?

"Estelle and I are just old friends. She'd like it to be more than that, but I'm not in love with her and I wouldn't hurt her like that."

For a man not used to explaining himself, Judson felt it important to set the record straight. As much as he hated to admit it, he did care what Carrie thought of him.

"It might come as a surprise to you, Carrie, but I don't sleep around. That's not the kind of example I want to set as a father. If anyone knows that actions speak louder than words, it's me."

Carrie didn't know that the specifics of that heartfelt statement included a lifetime of pain and disappointment. She only knew that beneath Judson's clear gaze, her doubts scattered like glittering bits of stardust. Ever since Brandy had informed Carrie that her father was engaged, she had been walking around with a great big rock dead-center in the middle of her chest. Relief shattered that rock into a million pieces and sent her heart soaring.

Unlike Scott, this man was neither a user nor a liar. If Judson was engaged to be married, clearly it was news to him. For some reason, Brandy had invented this whole story, and Carrie could see it only as a cry for help. One she desperately wanted to answer.

"Jud, your daughter told me in no uncertain terms that I was to stay away from you—that you were already spoken for."

"Why would she say such a thing when she knows it isn't true?" Judson was truly perplexed. Females, whatever their age, were a complete conundrum to him.

Carrie offered the only obvious answer. "Maybe because she hates me."

Her hurt tone implied that her concern was more than just professional.

Washakie's steady clip-clopping through the ice on the trail was the only other sound as she relayed the "jackalope marm" incident and ensuing conference she'd had with Brandy.

"Hold on," Judson directed, maneuvering the stallion onto a less-traveled trail.

Instinctively Carrie wrapped her arms more tightly around his waist.

"Didn't you tell me just the other night that you hated me?" he chided gently.

Embarrassed to have her own words thrown back at her, Carrie buried her face in the fur-lined collar of his coat. His neck smelled clean and kissable.

"That was different," she protested. "I was scared. And you know that I don't really hate you."

"Then you should know that Brandy doesn't really hate you, either. Has it ever occurred to you that she might simply feel threatened by our relationship?"

Carrie swallowed hard, knowing that this wouldn't

be easy to admit. "Actually, Brandy's not the only one who's scared. To be perfectly honest, my own feelings for you are pretty frightening. You might as well know the reason for my fears is that I once made the mistake of getting involved with my boss. It was disastrous. In fact, it ended up costing me my job."

Judson had wondered what the impetus had been for a woman like Carrie to suddenly move to such an isolated place. No wonder she had been so angry when she had discovered that he was chairman of the school board. No wonder his little practical joke had left such a sour taste in her mouth. He wanted to kick himself a hundred times over for his insensitivity.

At a loss for words, Judson found himself in the unenviable position of being pulled between the two strongest yet most vulnerable women in his life, Carrie and his daughter.

He had noticed that Brandy had been acting peculiar lately. When he'd come home late from the Open House the other day, she had been waiting up for him. The instant he'd opened the front door, she'd pounced on him demanding to know where he'd been. At the time Judson had dismissed her odd behavior as the onslaught of puberty, that perplexing condition that prompted her to lock herself in her bedroom one minute and throw her arms around his neck the very next.

Judson sighed philosophically. "Well, darlin', it looks like we're all going to need a little bit of time adjusting to one another and overcoming our personal fears." He certainly didn't exclude himself on this count.

Continuing on in a voice both tender and confident, he assured her, "I'll do my very best to earn your trust, and I don't doubt that sooner or later Brandy'll get used to the idea that she's going to have to share her daddy with another woman. Once she figures out that you're not out to steal all my love from her, she'll be all right.''

Carrie's breath caught in her throat. Had she heard him correctly? Had he actually used the word *love?*

Squinting against a sky too bright to look at with open eyes, Carrie felt her heart soar as high as the red-tailed hawk circling above. She rested her head against Judson's broad back and considered the future. Not so long ago she had thought herself too damaged by Scott's deception to ever open herself to another man's advances. Now she wasn't so sure.

Deep inside, Carrie knew both she and Judson carried a lot of emotional baggage that precluded either of them plunging headfirst into a relationship. Once she wished to dismiss the physical attraction she felt for Judson as being nothing more than a dream, a snowy, warm, wet dream that threatened to consume her body and soul and dissolve all her inhibitions and fears into a puddle of slush... Now in the dawn of a new day with her heart pumping out a wild, savage beat in time with Judson's own heart, Carrie no longer wanted to pretend that what she was feeling was anything less than love. True, aching, frightening, wonderful love.

Old fears about becoming involved with the boss dissolved beneath a sun that glistened on the melting snow like a field of diamonds. Judson was not Scott, she reminded herself. He wasn't even technically her boss; it wasn't as though he was in charge of evaluating her or anything. And hadn't he just admitted that he wasn't the kind of man who would use a woman just because she was willing and available?

There was something comfortably moral and upright about Judson. You could see it in the way he was raising his children. How rare was the man who would accept such responsibility, rising to the daily challenges of being a single father and provider. Carrie suspected that he would be as repulsed by Scott's underage choice of a sexual partner as she had been. Maybe even more so.

Carrie told herself that it was cowardly to allow past disappointments to keep her heart a prisoner forever. Promising to move forward in this relationship slowly, one step at a time, she knew she owed herself no less.

As they picked their way up the rock-studded hillside, it seemed to her that this land was too vast to be contained in the human heart. Somehow this simple life in the outback of Wyoming seemed more real than the one she had left behind. The sun here, unencumbered by smog and skyscrapers, nourished those plants strong enough to withstand its direct rays. Drinking in the warm sunshine, Carrie felt herself putting down deep roots.

Judson coaxed his horse through a narrow crevice in the face of the sheer canyon walls. Nature had cleverly obscured the opening. Reminded of the biblical reference of a camel passing through the eye of a needle, Carrie gasped in surprise as the aperture opened to a piece of heaven on earth.

A natural spring bubbled out of a cleft in the rocks to feed a small, crystalline pool surrounded on all sides by towering sandstone walls. Strange rock paintings of primitive creatures adorned the walls. Instinctively understanding she was on sacred ground, Carrie felt a shiver pass through her.

How many years ago had ancient travelers left their marks unobtrusively upon these walls in shades of charcoal and berry? She couldn't help but wonder what had inspired one particular drawing of what looked like a spaceman. The smudge of primitive fires still clung to the sandstone cliffs, and when Carrie closed her eyes she could almost hear the beat of primal drums.

Silently Judson dismounted. As he lifted his hands to her, Carrie abandoned herself to the sensation of falling, falling, falling…into a pair of sure arms. Feeling the impact of his arms crushing her body against his broad chest, she longed to taste his lips upon her own again. A sweet ache spread through her like wildfire, making her tingle all over in anticipation.

Judson noted that the sunlight caught in the wild tumble of her silken hair made Carrie look as pretty as a model. Sternly he reminded himself that this picture of youthful innocence was exactly the reason why he should stay far, far away from her. He knew his intentions were not the kind one should be entertaining about a respectable schoolteacher.

His troubled past alone would be enough to destroy her reputation, and if some of the community's more vocal bigots got wind of the fact that Carrie was romantically involved with a half-breed, he suspected they'd do their best to make her life a living hell. The thought drove a skewer right through his heart. He didn't want to be responsible for running off the best teacher who had ever graced the grounds of Harmony.

That thought, combined with the deep reverence he felt for this particular place, stopped him from taking her as he wished, this very instant, to couple beside these placid waters like animals uninhibited by unnatural constraints. But this was not some teenagers' lover's lane; it was holy ground. No matter how badly his body cried out for release, Judson would not violate honored tradition. Truly there was something mystical about this secluded hollow. This was the navel of the earth, connecting him to the land, to his ancestors, and ultimately to himself. In the breaching of a humpback whale, in the thunder of a herd of buffalo, in the strength of a cougar's awesome paw, in the proud toss of a wild horse's mane was the presence of the Great Spirit. It was a presence that shrouded this place in mystery and kept it hidden from sacrilegious interlopers.

"I'd appreciate it if you don't tell anyone about this place," he said softly. "It's not just that it's on my own private property, it's also part of my heritage, and I don't want a bunch of overzealous archaeologists disturbing the spirits."

"I won't," she promised.

That Judson had brought her here, an outsider in every sense, touched Carrie more deeply than she cared to admit. There were no words to express the overwhelming sense of serenity the place evoked in her. Clearly Judson remained faithful to his Native American heritage in his respect for Mother Earth. She felt truly privileged to share this hallowed ground with a man who managed to keep the very best of both of his cultures without compromising either.

The sincerity glistening in those eyes of satin green quelled any need Judson felt to press her further. The lessons of the past were but ashes in the wind. By inviting her here, Judson had opened his heart up to inspection. Like the consecrated waters bubbling forth from the hidden spring that fed this clear font, his lifeblood was similarly protected by sheer walls of stone. Etched upon them was an abiding reverence for the land itself, for the time-honored traditions of his ancestors, and for the love of a vanishing way of life.

Delving into eyes as trusting as a fawn's, Judson recognized the acceptance for which he had been searching all his life. A husky murmur caught in his throat as he pulled Carrie into the circle of his embrace. For a long time they remained entwined in one another's arms, paying homage to the past and welcoming the future.

Undisturbed by the outside world, they tasted the immeasurable potential of what could be—if only they could find the courage to overcome the obstacles in their way and learn to trust in one another.

Chapter Nine

Carrie and Judson savored the remaining moments that they shared in their enchanted sanctuary. Clearly something wonderful had happened today, something far beyond the physical attraction that both had fought since that first day when sparks had flown. Something beyond spoken words. Something echoed in the intimate bond of shared glances that excluded the rest of the world. Reveling in precious isolation, they lingered as long as possible before at last conceding that it was time to leave and proceed to Jud's hunting camp.

Bending and cupping his hands together, Judson instructed Carrie, "Put your left foot here and I'll help you mount up."

Though she would have preferred enjoying at her leisure the stimulating view that this pose provided her of the back of Judson's jeans, Carrie did as she was told.

"I'll ride behind you on the way back," he said, swinging up behind her. Doubting whether there was any polite way to explain how his manhood had been pressed too uncomfortably close to the saddle horn most of the way up here, Judson was glad when Carrie didn't ask for particulars.

As they took their leave, the sun cast a long shadow through the eyehole of the hidden opening. Awash in bright light, Carrie squinted against the sudden glare. She was completely caught off guard when the horse reared up in fright.

Poised on hind legs and pawing angrily at the air, a black bear was standing just outside the cleft in the mountain wall. A threatening roar echoed off sandstone. It was followed by a single expletive exploding from Judson's lips. He grabbed for the rifle in the scabbard attached to the saddle, but his hand grasped only empty air as both he and Carrie went flying. They weren't airborne for long. She landed upon a bed of soft pine needles, and Judson hit the ground with a sickening thud.

Carrie pulled herself into a sitting position to find herself looking over a square, tan nose and into a pair of wary eyes. Time stopped. Fear, dry and metallic, caked the roof of her mouth. Instinctively she understood that breaking eye contact would be taken as a sign of fear and would likely serve to provoke the bear. She didn't so much as blink, and an uneasy draw ensued.

The bear shook its head and growled low and deep. In response, a plaintive bawl arose nearby. Halfway up a scrub pine, a cub had its claws buried in soft bark and, in the confusion, appeared to have forgotten how to get down.

Lumbering over to her fractious toddler, Mamma Bear used the tree branches like a ladder to pull herself erect. Leaning her weight against the tree made it almost bend over double. Growing tired with all this unnecessary fuss, she nudged junior in the bottom to hasten him on his way. With a startled yelp, the cub hit the ground running.

Surprisingly agile for her four hundred plus pounds, Mamma herded her fugitive little fur ball toward one of the many caves pocketing the mountainside. The wide yawn that displayed a set of powerful jaws and large, gleaming teeth indicated it was time to get a start on the long winter's nap that would spare them the coldest months of the year. Tossing a final warning glance over her shoulder, Mamma Bear waggled off into the pine trees.

Eaten up with curiosity from its nose to its toes, the cub stopped momentarily to sniff at Judson's still form until an impatient, motherly bellow sent him scurrying into the timber with an obedient yip.

Had Judson not been lying motionless on the ground, the whole thing might have been comical. But Carrie wasn't laughing as she scrambled over to where he lay upon the cold, hard ground. His head was cradled between a jagged rock and a late-blooming patch of Indian Paint Brush. As bright as the flower's crimson petals, the melting snow was stained with his blood.

The world spun around Judson in slow motion. He wondered vaguely if this was the way it felt to be welcomed into heaven, wrapped in the arms of an angel. Feeling hot tears splash upon his face, he opened his eyes and squinted into a beautiful countenance haloed by the sun.

"It'll be all right," he assured Carrie with a half-cocked grin.

Like a flower opening itself to the sun, Judson felt the impact of this creature's beautiful smile spread throughout his body. He reached out for her, and finding her real indeed, pulled this healing angel into his arms, vowing to keep her there forever.

Reasoning that it couldn't be too bad if he was able to speak, Carrie sobbed in relief. She brushed away her tears with the back of her hand and asked, "How many fingers am I holding up?"

"Three."

Panic resurfaced in every pore of her body as she looked at the single finger she held in front of his eyes.

"Do you know where you are?" she asked.

"Heaven?"

Clearly Judson had a concussion. Carrie could only guess at its severity. Cussing the entire damned state of Wyoming for its snakes and bears and bitter cold and stubborn cowboys, Carrie railed against the hysteria that threatened to consume her. Remembering how Judson had been strong for her when she'd wrecked the snowmobile, she forced herself to remain calm.

How ironic it was that the only thing standing between Judson Horn and death was the same woman he'd once deemed too fragile to withstand the rigors of this rugged country. Unmindful of the cold, Carrie shed her coat, sweater and undershirt. Ripping the shirt into long strips, she wound them around Judson's head. Once satisfied that the bleeding had stopped, she redressed and attempted to get him to his feet.

It was like lifting a mountain.

"Come on," she urged, wrapping both arms around Judson's waist and trying to hoist him to his feet.

As if aware of the severity of the situation, Washakie cantered to his master's side and waited patiently. Judson grabbed for the saddle horn and missed. Shoving a shoulder beneath his buttocks, Carrie strained for all she was worth and somehow succeeded in draping him over the stallion like a sack of flour. Judson's eyes rolled back in his head. With an agonizing groan, he passed blissfully from consciousness.

It was a long way back, having to hold on to Judson and guide Washakie down the narrow trail, but there was no other way of transporting him safely down the mountainside. It took the better part of two hours to make it back to Harmony and another forty-five minutes for Carrie to careen down the switchbacks in her rickety pickup. At the speed with which she took those hairpin turns, she was surprised that she didn't kill them both before screeching to a halt outside the Lander Valley Medical Center.

Impatiently waiting in the lobby, Carrie marked time by monitoring the arthritic hands of the big clock on the wall. After what seemed like eternity, the doctor entered the room.

"I suppose you know that you're both damned lucky that you didn't end up spending the winter hibernating inside the belly of an old sow bear," Dr. Keats informed her with a glance over the rim of a pair of old-fashioned spectacles.

Carrie brushed off the comment as inconsequential. Worried that Judson may have suffered serious brain damage, she was in no mood for his Western bedside manner.

"How is he?" she demanded.

"Jud's as tough as an old piece of leather and as grizzly as a grizzly himself."

Chuckling at his play on words, he wiped his glasses on his hospital smock and donned a more serious bearing. "It took a dozen stitches to close up that gash in the back of his head. He's had his bell rung pretty hard, but in a week or so, I expect he'll be back to his old, ornery self. Till then he'll be sore, perhaps a little disoriented, and more'n likely mad as hell at being laid up.''

Carrie's body went limp with relief. She reached for the arm of a chair for support. "He's going to be all right then? There's no brain damage?''

"Oh, he'll have one humdinger of a headache that'll plague him for a day or two, but if you can assure me that you'll wake him up every hour tonight to check on him just to make sure that he doesn't slip into unconsciousness, I'll release him into your care immediately.''

Carrie squirmed uncomfortably in the silence that followed his prognosis. Didn't the good doctor realize in what a difficult position he was placing her? Granted, Judson needed someone to look after him and the children while he was incapacitated, but tongues were certain to wag if she were to temporarily move in with the chairman of school board, a man who just so happened to be the father of two of her pupils! Though the rest of the country might be progressively liberal, Carrie was well aware how decidedly conservative her little corner of it was. It didn't take a genius to realize that such action could well constitute grounds for dismissal.

As if reading her thoughts, Dr. Keats remarked, "It's not exactly like he's up for any hanky-panky.''

Frantically Carrie searched her mind for someone— anyone—to step in and help. A lusty image of Estelle Hanway popped into her head. Despite her fury at the Harvest Ball, Carrie felt certain the beautiful woman would jump at the chance to play Judson's nursemaid.

The thought caused her heart to flip-flop wildly inside her chest.

"I suppose I didn't just spend the longest day of my life hauling the man off the mountain just to abandon him now," she muttered into the doctor's bemused eyes.

If Carrie thought Judson was going to be happy at the prospect of having her at his beck and call, she was sorely disappointed. When she explained to him that she planned to be around to help out until he was back on his feet again, he bellowed in rage.

"I can take care of myself for God's sake! Been doing it since was I a kid."

Remembering the references to his alcoholic mother, Carrie assumed that his self-sufficiency stemmed from shouldering an adult's responsibility far too early in life. Though she longed to reach out and touch him with gentle compassion, she didn't dare. Such a proud man might easily mistake the gesture as a sign that she found him weak.

"I'm just relaying the doctor's orders," she responded with a smile that felt tight over her teeth. "With you out of commission for a while, somebody's going to have to take care of the twins anyway. I doubt if it'll be much more work looking after you, too, but if you insist, you're welcome to stay in the hospital for just as long as you'd like."

Recognizing that same stubborn set to her jaw as when Carrie had told him in no uncertain terms that she wasn't about to turn tail and go back to Chicago without putting up a fight, Judson knew arguing was useless— despite the fact that the whole situation was a powder keg just waiting to be lit.

Considering Brandy's disturbing behavior in the classroom lately, there was bound to be hell to pay when he brought Carrie home for a "sleep over." Judson could only imagine how Cowboy would to react when he discovered that his father was as smitten with his pretty teacher as he, not to mention the fact that Judson himself was certain to be in a state of permanent arousal with this confounding, lovely creature catering to his every need. He could think of no better prescription for utter pandemonium.

Unfortunately, Judson had little choice in the matter. For the first time in over two decades, he needed to rely on another human being for help. Considering that he had always thought she was the one who needed looking after, it galled him to think that Carrie Raben, of all people, would have to take care of him. This sudden role reversal hurt his pride something awful. Up until now he had seen himself as the strong one, whose job was to show this fresh greenhorn the fundamentals of surviving in the woolly West. How quickly enigmatic Ms. Raben had turned the tables on him. The fact that a big man like himself was suddenly reduced to helplessness was humiliating, to say the least.

Along with the pill the nurse handed him, Judson Horn swallowed his pride.

Before leaving the hospital, Carrie placed a call to the children, who had been spending the day at the neighbors'. After explaining the situation to Mrs. Milford, she asked if the family would mind feeding Cowboy and Brandy supper. That would give her time enough to get Judson to bed before the twins got home.

A hot blush swept over her at the thought of tucking Judson in. For the millionth time she wondered how in the world she was ever going to manage this. Just being in this man's presence was enough to set her on fire.

Judson slept most of the way home, leaving Carrie to her own thoughts. Having passed by but never under the huge log archway that marked the entrance to the Blue Sky Lodge, she was unprepared for the size and grandeur of Judson's ranch. Highlighted against a spectacular Wyoming sunset, his home was nestled in a grove of pine trees. As impressive as the land from which it was carved, the spacious stone building was an integral part of the surrounding countryside. The scene emoted an aura of peaceful tranquility that contrasted dramatically with the turmoil Carrie was feeling inside.

Awakening her patient from his medicated sleep, she announced brightly, "Wake up! We're here!"

Carrie helped him from the vehicle, insisting that he lean on her for support. "Easy does it," she murmured as they tottered up the flagstone walk. *Easy does it... Easy does it...* she repeated to her racing heart.

Finding the front door locked, she looked at Judson askance.

"Key's in my pants' pocket," was his terse reply.

Was she merely imagining the hoarse, gritty tone of his voice? Feeling the now-familiar heat radiating from the center of her body, she pushed aside any prim-and-proper ideas about how ladies were supposed to behave. After all, hadn't the doctor assured her that his patient wasn't up for any hanky-panky? Carrie plunged her hands into his two front pockets and fished out a ring laden with keys—but not before feeling the arousal of his manhood, large and obvious against her fingertips. Injured or not, this man wasn't about to let her forget about his overt sexual appeal. Nervously she fumbled with several keys before finally coming up with the right one.

Flipping on the porch light illuminated Judson's weakened condition. His eyes were glazed over, his face was a ghastly hue, and a grimace curled his lips.

Pain pierced Carrie's heart with the accuracy of an arrow. Her concern for Judson's well-being outweighed everything else. Community mores, her job, Brandy's disapproval, her reputation—all meant nothing in light of the fact that Judson needed her.

Carrie led him into the house and turned on a light. She was astounded at the immensity of the living room in which she stood. The central feature of the room was a fireplace built of the same stately gray stone as the house itself. The floor was polished wood with Arapaho rugs scattered throughout.

"Bedroom's up there." Judson pointed.

Even under such benign circumstances the words sent a flame racing along her nerve endings. The illicit thoughts she entertained as she studied the polished banistered staircase leading from the living room to the loft would surely make a nun blush. Admonishing herself for her lack of self-control, Carrie wondered how Judson was ever going to manage that flight of stairs. She thought about simply making up the couch for him, but considering the possibility that he might wake up disoriented in the night, attempt to maneuver his way up the stairs alone and end up hurting himself, she quickly dismissed that idea. What if he somehow managed to make his way up to his room and stumbled upon her asleep in his bed? The very thought centered a quiver low in her stomach.

Carrie was shaken from her dewy fantasy by the realization that she needed to get Judson to bed as quickly as possible. Although he had all his senses, he was groggy from the pain pills the doctor had prescribed.

Tackling the stairs together as a team, Judson held on to the banister with one hand and his caretaker's slender shoulders with the other. Aware that he was trying his best not to crush her beneath his weight, Carrie knew how hard it was for such an independent man to rely upon anyone else—and her in particular, the outsider whom he had openly denounced as being unfit to persevere upon his turf.

Opening the door to Judson's bedroom, Carrie felt her already racing heartbeat quicken. In the middle of the room sat a king-size brass bed. It was impossible not to imagine snuggling naked with Judson between warm sheets, serenaded by the sound of a roaring fireplace below. With difficulty, she donned a professional nurselike attitude, pretending that she wasn't bothered in the least by what she had to do next.

Turning back the covers, she helped him to the edge of the bed and announced coolly, "Let me help you out of your pants."

"Listen here." Judson's husky voice had the same effect upon the blood coursing through her veins as a pint of smooth whiskey. "I'm too old to be tucked in with just a kiss on the forehead. There's only one reason I'll let you take my pants off, and I think you know what it is."

Carrie's heart careened against her chest as a wet heat spread through her. Her eyes were drawn to the worn fly of his jeans. What she saw there left little doubt that his concussion had not affected the other working parts of his body.

Her hands were sweaty, her heart was hammering out a lusty song, and her body felt heavy and sweet with desire. She was sorely tempted to put that masculine boast to the test.

How, she wondered miserably, was she ever going to survive her nursing internship with such a testosterone-driven hunk of a patient with either her heart or her reputation intact?

Giving him her best I'm-in-charge-now look, she calmly informed her patient, "You just do as you're told, and we'll see about attending to your 'other' needs later."

The slow smile Judson gave her as he stretched his long body across the bed threatened to obliterate any sense of decency Carrie ever had.

Since the logical place to start was with his boots, she grasped one worn boot firmly in both hands and pulled…and pulled…and pulled. Clearly this wasn't going to be easy. Placing the heel of the boot against her stomach, she gave another tug. When the boot came off in her hands, she was thrown off balance and fell back against the wall.

Woozy as he was, Judson had never been so aroused in all of his life as he was by the sight of this sweet thing struggling to divest him of his boots. She was so adorable it made his mouth water with wanting her. Little did it matter that his head was pounding a rhythm akin to ancient war drums when the throbbing in the lower half of his body demanded his immediate attention. Though his natural inclination was to dismiss his reaction as nothing more than a bad case of lust, deep in his heart Judson knew that it was far more than that.

He wondered how he could possibly defend his heart against a woman capable of staring down a bear, an animal traditionally honored for its valor in Indian lore and legend. That this remarkable woman had been able to connect with sister bear on some metaphysical plane was as mystical as the bond that connected them. Judson knew only that he was no more able to break that bond by an act of simple willpower than he was able to stop himself from breathing.

As she swept a stray lock from her eyes with the back of her hand, he was struck by the loveliness of that face, flushed with exertion. Her eyes were so wide and wondrous that he felt certain the mysteries of the entire universe were contained within their depths. By the time his tousle-haired nymph had his second boot off, Judson was on the verge of exploding with desire.

With fingers that felt thick and clumsy, Carrie began the process of unbuttoning his shirt. Her remonstrance to stop them from shaking was for naught. Judson took her trembling hands into his own and brought them to his lips. Slowly she raised her eyes to meet his and saw the passion glistening there. The raw need.

Shirt hanging open to reveal his smooth, muscular chest, Judson pulled her hands down to cover his heart. It was a gesture so tender, so intimate, that its simple eloquence brought tears to her eyes.

He slipped his arms around her waist and pulled her atop him on the bed. Running his hands beneath her sweater, he captured the creamy swells of her breasts in the palms of his hands. Judson thrust aside any lingering doubts he had about the past. The sound of Carrie's whimper centered his need directly on the present. This all-consuming desire was too much to fight, and the truth of the matter was that he didn't want to fight it anymore. This wasn't his fickle high-school sweetheart he was holding in his arms; it was Carrie, all sweetness and ripe womanhood, exploring his body with hungry need.

This couldn't be her boss, Carrie thought to herself as Judson tasted the sensitive hollow of her neck with his tongue. This was the man she loved. No past experience or job-related reasoning could alter the irrefutable fact that despite her best efforts to the contrary, she had fallen helplessly, hopelessly, in love with Judson Horn. To deny it was to deny fate itself.

His mouth sought hers, and he traced her soft pliant lips with the tip of his tongue. Feeling the quickening thud of his heart against her palm, she submitted to what was surely her destiny. The deep ache inside her burst into an iridescent glow that radiated throughout every cell in her body, blotting out all reason. It felt so very right, and her need was so urgent, so overpowering. Shivering with desire too long suppressed, Carrie moaned a soft surrender.

He continued to brush his lips over hers in a provocative prelude that left her quivering in awe. Melting beneath the sweet exploration of his tongue, Carrie blindly responded. Her hands devoured the smooth plane of his chest. Hungry for more, she sought the broad expanse of his shoulders, slipping his shirt down his arms, ridding him of it entirely. She caressed the breadth of his back.

It took a moment for her mind to register what those raised ridges of flesh beneath her fingertips actually were. Judson's back was hideously scarred. "As tough as old leather," the doctor had said. Apparently someone had treated Judson Horn as little more than just that.

Her eyes filled with tears as she broke away from his kisses. "Who did this to you?" she demanded in a hoarse whisper.

The answer to that question came from behind her. "Somebody just like you...."

Chapter Ten

Like an adolescent caught necking by a local police officer, Carrie jumped off the bed. Red-faced, she wheeled around to face Brandy, who was standing in the doorway with her arms akimbo and her eyes ablaze.

"Why would you say that? I would never do anything to hurt your father. I—I love him!" she stammered in self-defense.

At this heartfelt proclamation, Brandy's eyes narrowed to slits. "It was love of a white woman that almost got him killed before!"

With that, the girl slammed the door and raced down the hallway to her room. Torn between her desire to stay with Judson and to chase after his distraught daughter, Carrie was relieved when the matter was settled with a gentle entreaty.

"Let her be for the time being. You and I need to talk."

Looking into eyes of shimmering green was to peer into Carrie's very soul, Judson realized. This beautiful woman was far too guileless to hide her emotions behind the kinds of barriers that he had so skillfully erected around his own heart. It was impossible for Carrie to willfully hurt anyone she loved. And if he could believe his own ears, he had just heard her admit to loving him.

It was a miracle. Something too good to be true.

Fearing that she would dismiss his apprehension about the consequences of racially blended relationships as trifling, Judson wanted her to understand the magnitude of his concern. It was imperative if they were to ever commit to a future together.

But how could he dredge up a past so willfully suppressed for so long? Holding out his hand, Judson pulled Carrie down beside him on the bed. At last the time had come to open the pages of a book too long sealed shut.

Longing to ease his pain, Carrie offered Judson the solace of her body. Remembering Estelle Hanway's words about the brothers who hadn't taken kindly to their sister's involvement with a half-breed, she ran her hands along the width of that scarred back and massaged his knotted flesh.

The scars you can see ain't nothing compared to those you can't.

At the time those words seemed cryptic; Carrie had thought them spoken in a state of drunken confusion. Suddenly they made perfect sense.

"I told you that my mother was an alcoholic," he began quietly. "I didn't tell you how very much like you she was—beautiful, kind and gentle."

Judson paused to study Carrie's face between his hands, her features more precious than the most exquisite jewels.

"When she told the man she loved she was pregnant, he refused to accept the child as his own. Unwilling to admit siring a bastard breed, Mr. High-and-Mighty Arthur Christianson turned his back on us both and pretended we simply didn't exist.

"A mongrel dog feels more responsibility to its offspring than my father did. Though money was never an issue for him, he didn't contribute so much as a dime to our welfare," he stated contemptuously.

All the years of locking the past up in his heart hadn't lessened Judson's pain any. It glittered in his eyes.

"Still, Mother never gave up hope that her shining white knight would someday return to claim me as his son, to restore me to my rightful 'throne.' Her people interpreted that obstinacy as a denial of her own kind. Nobody protested her decision to keep my name off the Indian rolls; there were plenty of full-bloods who needed financial help more than any whelp breed. Cursed by my Indian brothers for my blue eyes and whites for the color of my skin, I was accepted by neither."

The words themselves evoked memories of cruel, childish taunts, of blackened eyes and bloody noses, of threats more often than not carried out with the security of numbers on their side. Hearing the raspy sound of his own voice cracking, Judson struggled to master his emotions.

"We went it alone for years, living in a hovel that caused the authorities to periodically inquire about health conditions."

Tears glistening in her eyes, Carrie longed to give Judson permission to wrap the past back up in its fragile cocoon. But she couldn't. Not when she knew a catharsis was necessary before deep healing could begin.

She doubted whether he noted the gentle pressure of her hand squeezing his. Lost in the mist of the past, Judson was far, far away.

"Lord knows, she tried hard to be a good parent, but the day she found relief in a bottle, my mother crawled inside and never found her way back out."

With a dry, self-deprecating cough, Judson spared himself no measure of mercy.

"I was the world's youngest enabler. I did whatever it took to cover up. Stole, lied, denied. Missed lots of school trying to keep things together. Terrified that Social Services would declare my mother unfit and take me away from her, I did everything I could to hide our problems from the world. Little did I know that by not making my mother face her problems I was only contributing to them."

"You were only a little boy! You're being too hard on yourself," Carrie protested.

"A little boy who came home from school one day to find his mother dead."

Judson's voice was like the wind whistling over the desolate stretch of his weathered heart. "To a certain degree, I'll always blame myself for her death."

The little cry of pain Carrie heard was her own. Her heart swelled with empathy for the child who had borne such an unfathomable load upon his narrow shoulders. If only there was some way to get the man to forgive himself.

Having seen the same look reflected in numerous social workers' faces, Judson loathed the pity glistening in Carrie's eyes. It was almost too much to bear.

"The next several years a string of well-intentioned psychologists and social workers tried to 'absorb me into the system.' But ultimately the system rejected me.

Nobody wanted to adopt a mixed-breed teenager with an attitude.

"Most of the foster families I lived with just wanted the extra money the government gave them for housing me. It was even worse in the families where I did form an emotional attachment to my foster brothers and sisters. I never stayed long in one place, and I learned fast that caring led straight to heartache."

That certainly explained a lot to Carrie. No wonder he had flinched at her recommendation to get Brandy some counseling. Tenderly tracing the scars on his back, she massaged the corded muscles. Her trembling fingers fluttered like butterflies against his flesh.

Bitterly self-conscious about the scars that curled around his back like so many writhing snakes, Judson was surprised that he did not recoil from her touch. Heightened by the eroticism of her gentle caresses, his body reacted as if she were playing a worn, well-loved guitar.

When he resumed speaking, his voice was little more than a husky whisper. "I was well on the road to reform school when Cheryl Sue McLeashe started making goo-goo eyes at me in high school."

A self-effacing smirk underscored his quick synopsis. "It was the typical story—a perky socialite falling for the bad boy renegade. Convinced by the system that I was unlovable, I'd made up my mind not to have anything to do with her. But Cheryl Sue was determined to prove that status and race really didn't matter to her. Like a fool, I hoped to break out of the destructive pattern that marked not only my own family history but the history of a nation."

His voice was devoid of any emotion as he relayed

the milestone that had changed the course of his life. "We eloped right after graduation."

A lump the size of a fist formed in Carrie's throat. It was foolish, she knew, to be intimidated by ghosts from the past, but what woman can compete with a man's first love? Anger against the girl who had first laid claim upon Judson welled up in her heart. However genuine her motives, Cheryl Sue had stolen Judson's innocence—and his faith in love. Had she rendered him incapable of ever trusting his heart again?

"You can tell by my back just how well her family took the news. Didn't matter to her brothers that Cheryl Sue claimed she was in love with me. All that mattered was that I was a breed—and as such a totally unacceptable marriage partner for their sister.

"They whipped me until I passed out. Like Brandy said, they would have probably killed me if Cheryl Sue hadn't thrown herself at them, begging for my life... threatening to take her own if they didn't stop."

The barriers were down in those haunted blue eyes that had marked Judson an outcast from birth. In their cerulean depths, Carrie spied a glimpse of hell.

"Unfortunately," he continued with the honest reflection born of hindsight, "it turned out Cheryl Sue was more in love with the romantic notion of sampling forbidden fruit than she ever was with me. A young idealist, she was completely unprepared for the social ostracism that comes with mixed marriages. Her daddy had our marriage annulled almost before it was official. And I'm told he tried to make her get rid of the babies she was carrying, too. But to her credit, Cheryl stood up to that old devil, carrying the twins to term without his blessing.

"They were barely a week old when I found them

on my front step, two tiny angels bundled up in matching pink and blue blankets.''

Judson's eyes softened with the memory before turning the color of armor-piercing bullets. "Left on my front porch like somebody's garbage."

Though his rage was under control, it was clear to Carrie that it had not dissipated with the passage of years.

"I was young and in pretty bad shape at the time, and I couldn't imagine having anything so little and innocent and needy totally dependent on me. To be honest, there were times I didn't think we'd make it. Times when all we had was each other."

It was easy to see how Judson's children had bonded so completely to him. How Brandy could come to see any romantic interest shown her father as an infringement upon her sole, proprietary turf. Though Carrie wished there was some way to simply make Judson's anguish disappear, the truth was, the past could not be undone. Considering what he'd just revealed, it was inconceivable that he would simply throw his heart wide open to her raw, reckless admission of love.

Still Carrie wouldn't have retracted it if she could. Even if he spurned her, demanding she get out of his life for good, she knew that silencing the fact that she was a woman in love wouldn't lessen that earth-shattering reality one iota.

Outside a coyote howled a baleful tune to the rising moon as Carrie considered a lifetime of loving a man so deeply scarred. There were her wounds to consider, as well. Though not as visible as Judson's, she, too, was marred by the past, haunted by her own demons. Could love really triumph over so much mutual pain?

As if reading her thoughts, Judson stepped into the

deep grass of those gentle eyes. "Sweetheart, I don't think you've fully considered the repercussions of loving a breed."

"Shh..."

Putting a finger to his lips, Carrie shushed him in an act so sweet and sensual that it turned his protests to a feral growl. He took her hands into his own and kissed their open palms.

"Don't you realize that just being here with me jeopardizes your standing in this community? You deserve a better life than a crazy blue-eyed breed with two mixed-up kids."

"Let me be the judge of that," Carrie countered with a stubborn lift of her chin.

Undoubtedly there were obstacles to overcome: his past and her own. But, after all, history was only history. The shadows of the past were behind them; the sunlit fields of the future lay ahead. Judson was no longer the boy he once was. He was a man with the courage to put family first, and she, a woman strong enough to fight for what she wanted.

Opening her hands to encompass their tasteful surroundings, she gently reminded him, "You're not such a bad catch after all. I wouldn't exactly describe this as the 'hovel' of your childhood. And don't forget, it was the people of this community who elected you to a seat on the school board."

Judson flinched at the conclusion to which she had jumped. His wry smile was tinged with derision. "You can chalk all that up to my old man. The only good thing he ever did for me was to up and die."

Carrie tried to understand Judson's callousness as he tried to disenchant her with the unpleasant facts of his life.

"Believe me, nobody was more surprised than me to find out that Arthur Christianson left me his entire estate. Funny how his death bought me what he refused me during his life—a modicum of respectability."

This startling disclosure didn't stop Carrie from rushing to his support. "But you've got to remember that you're the one who's held on to it. Surely you don't think you were elected by your peers to be chairman of the board out of pity!"

The bold spark dancing in those emerald eyes communicated complete belief in him. Had Cheryl Sue but been able to have trusted him even a fraction such as this, Judson was sure his life would not have been so riddled with self-doubt, recriminations and regrets.

Vowing not to let pride smother the wisdom of his heart, he wrapped his arms tightly around Carrie and pulled her close.

"You're a remarkable woman," he murmured into the soft cascade of her hair.

In that instant Judson realized the only thing standing between him and happiness was his own fear. Like a cat, he had bared his claws for so long that he had forgotten how to purr, how to trust in innate goodness when it was staring him right in the face. Truly as beautiful on the inside as the outside, Carrie Raben was woman enough to take whatever the world had to throw at her. Judson couldn't believe that he had been willing to allow a past marred by other people's bigotry to come between him and the best thing that was ever going to happen in his life.

His lips claimed hers in a kiss borne of desperation and fate. Soft. The parting of those exquisitely soft lips to accept all that he had to offer aroused him fully, invoking an insatiable longing Judson had never before felt. The reciprocal thrust of her tongue against his own almost sent him over the edge.

Growling deep in his throat, Judson reveled in the seductive curves that molded so perfectly to his hard, angular body. Unable to get enough, his hands moved hungrily over her, his savage virility threatening to conquer the virgin innocence that had captivated him from the very first day he had been entrusted with her well-being. Knowing that Carrie was not the kind of woman to accept intimacy on a merely physical plane, Judson knew where this was going.

Straight from the bedroom to the altar.

And suddenly to his great surprise that didn't seem like such a bad idea. He hadn't seen very many marriages that were made in heaven. His own wasn't much of a yardstick; his own father had disavowed the institution completely. Not so long ago Judson had thought that it would be enough to have a relationship without any permanency or bonds. Now he wasn't so sure. Having finally found the only woman he wanted in his life, he wasn't willing to accept her on a part-time-only basis. He peeked twenty years into the future and saw them holding hands together on the front porch with grandchildren clustered at their feet.

Judson smiled at the thought. Whatever it took to convince Carrie to marry him, how ever long it took to break down her fears, he was going to win her over to his way of thinking.

Feeling the impact of his hard body pressed against her, Carrie did not resist as Judson's mouth closed upon hers. She responded with her entire being to the power of his kiss. Never before had she felt anything so wild, so strong. Quivering, she twined her fingers in the silky, thick darkness of his hair. The muscles on the arms that held her were ropes of sinew, his chest a broad, smooth wall of strength. Running her hands across that bare chest, she felt the quickening thud of his heart against her open palm. It matched hers beat for beat.

It felt so very right, and their shared need was so very urgent. Passion leapt between them like a flame threatening to blaze out of control. Enveloped in the loving embrace of Judson's arms, Carrie allowed herself to envision her life with a man who was strong enough to lean on and gentle enough to trust.

The echo of the front door slamming shut reverberated throughout the house. Reason slowly returned to eyes that were dazed and heavy-lidded.

"Brandy!" they mouthed simultaneously.

Given the girl's volatile nature, both worried that, in a desperate ploy for attention, she just might do something dramatic. Something dangerous.

Clearly before things went any further between the two of them, matters had to be settled with that live grenade presently masquerading as a twelve-year-old girl.

Considering that Carrie didn't have the faintest notion of what to do next, she was surprised at how calm and resolute her voice sounded as she announced to Judson, "You get some rest. I'll go after her."

Stepping from the security of Judson's bedroom into a battleground, Carrie noticed that the door to Cowboy's room was wide open. He was sitting on the edge of his bed wearing a very worried expression.

Not wanting to invade his personal space, she queried from the door, "Are you okay?"

He met her question with one of his own. "Is Dad going to be all right?"

How patiently he had been waiting for word on his father. Carrie could no more refuse those pleading blue eyes than she could stop her heart from beating. Brandy's tantrum could wait just a minute more. This was equally important.

Realizing how scared he must be, Carrie assured him as she crossed the room, "He's going to be just fine, sweetheart."

From the rapt expression that lit up his face when she came to sit beside him on the bed, it was apparent that at least one of Judson's children did not perceive her as the enemy. His crush on her was as obvious as the sun that warmed the mountain hollows, and just as sustaining.

Grateful for the warm reception, Carrie ruffled the boy's hair affectionately. With a smile so like his father's, he tugged firmly on her heart.

The walls of Cowboy's private domain were covered with posters of horses and his own original artwork, the floor littered with video games, sports cards and *Western Horseman* magazines. A worn guitar was propped against the windowsill, and a live spider imprisoned in a jelly jar resided beside an artfully displayed arrangement of native arrowheads.

Never had Carrie felt so immediately at home as amid the eclectic clutter of this room. She felt like visiting royalty as a boy with shining eyes the same astounding shade of blue as his father's shyly mumbled, "I'm glad you're here."

Wrapping his arms around his teacher's waist, he emphasized his sincerity by squeezing as hard as he could.

"Me, too," Carrie replied, fighting back the tears that came unbidden to her eyes.

"Do you know where Brandy went?" she asked, forcing herself to focus on the crisis at hand.

"Out to the barn to saddle up Dolly. I told her it was too late to go riding, but she never listens to me."

It was getting dark outside. If Brandy got it into her head to take off, it would be almost impossible to track her down. There had to be a million places on a ranch this size for a cagey twelve-year-old to hide.

"I've got to catch her," she told Cowboy, hurrying from the room.

"You'll be back?" he asked. "Won't you?"

Carrie stopped in midstride. "I promise."

Her heart swelled with affection for the child whose wide eyes reflected the fear that she might vanish without a trace—just like the mother he never knew. For a long time Carrie had known that what she felt for Judson's children was more than just teacherly concern. Since that fateful first day of school, she had felt connected to the twins on some deeper level. Brandy, with her hot temper, and Cowboy, with his spontaneous friendliness, had somehow instantly gotten under her skin—just like their father.

Other than complete abandonment to loving the whole darn family, Carrie could think of no other cure for this extraordinary malady.

Brandy was putting her foot in the stirrup when Carrie walked into the barn. It was apparent from her red-rimmed eyes and puffy face that she had been crying.

"Whadda you want?" Brandy muttered, pulling herself into the saddle.

"Just to talk to you."

"Why don't you save it for my dad? Maybe that conk on the head made him forget about what happened the last time he trusted one of your kind. It's already made him forget about his family."

Her angry tone was underscored by the quivering of her lower lip. Carrie felt her heart constrict in empathy. To any twelve-year-old the possibility of losing her father to an accident—or another woman—would be overwhelming. To one already abandoned by her mother, it would be tantamount to the end of the world. After a lifetime of having her father to herself, it was inevitable that Brandy would feel betrayed about him becoming romantically involved.

"You know that isn't true," Carrie gently responded. "I've never met anyone who cared more for his family than your father."

"Then why don't you just leave us alone?" Brandy reined her horse sharply toward the open doors and shouted, "Can't you see we don't need you?"

Carrie felt the force of the girl's words like a fist to her gut. She grabbed the reins to halt the horse, struggling to respond in a tone that belied her pain.

Adjusting the medical terminology to a sixth-grade level, she relayed the doctor's diagnosis.

"So you see your father needs someone to look after him for a couple days—just until we're sure he's over his concussion. I'm just here to help out temporarily."

"I told you we don't need your help. I can take care of Daddy by myself."

"Are you prepared to take care of your father for the rest of his life then? Because if you intend to keep your daddy from ever falling in love again with anyone else but you, that's exactly what you're setting yourself up

for. Do you understand how unfair that is to him and
to you?''

Misgiving glistened in the girl's dark eyes as she
studied the teacher. Lashing out in fear, Brandy replied
sullenly, ''You're so sure you know what's best for all
of us, don't you? Well, you don't. You don't know
anything about what it's like to grow up part Indian in
a white man's world. You don't know what it's like
being dumped by your white mother or what it's like
being teased because your half-breed father inherited his
seat on the school board. You don't know anything
about me at all!''

''I know you're scared, Brandy, and that you're hid-
ing behind a worn-out excuse to justify your anger. This
doesn't have anything whatsoever to do with me being
white. It has to do with you wanting to keep everything
in your life the way it is right now.''

Carrie's voice rose with the passion of her statement.
''There are a lot of things in life you can't control and
trying to keep your father hobbled is just selfish.''

Brandy reacted with the disdain only a budding teenager can truly master with the complete assurance that
everyone else in the world is mistaken. ''You're the
selfish one, not me. You've stolen all our land and now
you're out to steal my daddy!''

Carrie sighed. Was there any way of opening such a
closed mind?

''*I* didn't steal your land. *I* didn't whip your father.
And just like you didn't have anything to do with your
mother's leaving, *I* didn't have anything to do with the
subjugation of the Indian by the white man. That's all
history, Brandy, and you're far too smart to use it as a
convenient excuse to hold on to your pain, to never have
to make something of yourself.''

Brandy didn't want to listen. She reacted like a cat arching its back and hissing at its enemy. "If you're staying here, then I'm leaving!"

Carrie realized that she was getting nowhere fast. She loved Judson, and she loved his children. But it was hopeless to think she would ever be accepted into the circle of this family's love. She was an unwelcome intruder standing at the window, looking in from the outside and aching for the familial bonds so obviously lacking in her own solitary life.

A heavy sigh bespoke her utter weariness. "You win, Brandy. I'll leave so you can have your daddy all to yourself. But before I do, there's something you need to understand. I love your father, and I love you and Cowboy, too. *Nothing* you can say or do will ever change that fact. I never wanted to steal anything from you, just to share your love as a family. Your father's a good man, and he deserves to be loved—just like you do."

Addressing the girl as an equal, Carrie spoke with complete honesty. "Don't you understand there is more than one way to whip a man?"

A stricken look crossed Brandy's features.

"When you wake your father in an hour, please let him know that I'm gone," Carrie said as she turned and slowly walked out of their lives.

Chapter Eleven

"Daddy, wake up!"

Brandy was on the verge of hysteria.

Several hours had passed since Ms. Raben had driven down the road. Afraid to explain to her father how she had been the cause of Carrie's leaving, Brandy had deliberately ignored the directive to awaken him every hour. But as the clock struck midnight, she had finally come to admit that she would be unable to get any sleep without first checking on her father. With a martyr's sigh, Brandy had tossed back the covers and tiptoed down the hallway.

Suddenly the consequences of her father's wrath faded into insignificance. Judson lay inert, impervious to all attempts to wake him.

Shaking him by the shoulders, she begged him to come to. "Please. Please. Oh please, Daddy, wake up!"

Gulping air like a drowning man, Judson at last came to in a confused stupor. He shook his head to chase away the fog. Bad mistake. He hurt all over.

Had he been caught looking the wrong way in an avalanche? Run over by a Brahma bull? Leveled by a pair of bewitching emerald eyes?

Tears spattered his face. Judson opened his eyes to see his daughter, pale-faced and distraught, looking down at him as if she were viewing him in a coffin.

"What's the matter?" he groaned, squinting against the overhead light.

Brandy's only response was a heartfelt sob of relief as she wrapped her arms around his neck and proceeded to choke him half to death.

Slowly Judson's head began to clear. Bits of memory floated through his mind like debris upon an inky sea. A she bear and her cub. Washakie rearing. The hospital. Carrie's sudden, sweet espousal of love. Her promise to be there for him when he woke up....

"Where's Carrie?" he mumbled.

Again Brandy's response was tearful silence.

Pulling himself to a sitting position, Judson grabbed a pain pill from the bed stand and swallowed it without benefit of water. Doubting whether the problem was with his daughter's hearing, he repeated, "I asked you, where's Carrie?"

Brandy dared not make him ask again. "Gone." Uttered with a teary hiccup, the word stretched into more than one syllable.

Instantly Judson was wide-awake and alert. "What happened?" he demanded, his eyes as clear and piercing as scalpels.

"It's all my fault. I drove her away..." she began with a sniffle.

By the time Brandy had finished the telling, Judson was on his feet, scrambling for his pants and the keys to his vehicle. Somewhere in between the part where

his daughter admitted her insecurities about losing him
and the part where she threw her arms around him begging for forgiveness, Judson and Brandy reached a joy-
ful discovery: what they both really wanted was one
another's happiness.

Judson assured her that his affection for Carrie did
not diminish his love for her. And then Brandy warmed
to the idea of having a woman around to help her with
those "girl problems" that puberty thrusts upon even
the most unwilling tomboys and makes single fathers
long for medieval solutions like chastity belts. Brandy
confessed that she, in fact, liked Carrie very much, not
only as a teacher but as a friend who had been honest
enough to make her face herself in the mirror.

A friend who would probably make one terrific
mother—if only given half a chance.

When Jud, full of determination, headed for the door,
Brandy called after him. "I'd like to go with you—if it
isn't too late."

If it isn't too late...

What had his stiff-necked pride cost him? The prospect of waking up every day for the rest of his life in
a house devoid of Carrie's loving presence filled Judson's heart with a rush of cold, chilling wind. The loneliness that had consumed so much of his life was replaced by a hunger to join his life with another.

If it isn't too late...

What if the door slammed in his face and the bolt
slid shut? Worse, what if Carrie had finally come to her
senses and was packing her things right now?

The answer was obvious. He would just have to beat
the door down and prepare to grovel like never before
in his entire life.

He wasn't about to let bad timing hold him back for an instant.

"Go get your brother," he commanded. "And hurry."

Carrie wondered if it were possible to perish of loneliness in the span of a single, endless night. She stared at her bedroom ceiling and thought about Judson. All alone in that big house, with a concussion and two kids: both as needy as their father. Would either of them ensure that their father took his medicine on time? Could Cowboy possibly understand that she had been forced to break her promise not to leave? Given the ultimatum to leave or make ready for Brandy to run away and desert her family, had there been a choice? When Judson came to, would he simply assume that, like his ex-wife, she had taken a powder when things got rough?

Repeatedly Carrie threw Judson and his children out of her mind, but like a contrary old hound, they would sneak right back in.

How dare they make her fall in love with each and every one of them and then lock her out when she got too close? Carrie tried to milk that sense of outrage for all it was worth. After all, anger had held her afloat when Scott had shown his true colors. It had helped her hold her chin high despite the ringing taunts of those venomous teenagers. Anger had been the impetus for moving out West and starting her life anew. Rage could be turned into something positive.

But try as she might, Carrie couldn't remain angry. Not with Judson. Or with his children. Brandy was, after all, only a child. A child abandoned by her mother for nothing more than the fraction of Indian blood that ran in her veins. It was not unreasonable that she would see

Carrie as another white intruder out to undermine the only point of stability in her life—her father.

Nor could she blame Judson himself for failing to meet her sudden avowal of love with an equally impetuous, romantic overture. A man as deeply scarred by love as Judson had been could hardly be expected to embrace such a confounding concept ever again.

What Carrie *was* feeling was a deep, abiding sense of loss, a pain so intense it left her blissfully numb. Inside her was a hurt big enough to qualify as a black hole. She was having a hard time accepting the fact that love alone was simply not enough to heal the wounds or chase away the fears that shaped the man and his family. She had done her very best to try to make Brandy see reason, and she had failed. The girl had made her feelings perfectly clear. And Judson himself had been equally candid about the way he felt about marriage. Not that she could blame him given his past history with the institution.

Carrie knew there was no chance of ever being accepted into the tightly knit tapestry of the Horn family. The helplessness of it was infuriating. The sooner she accepted that fact, the sooner she could get on with her life.

Though she told herself that she still had her career, Carrie knew no job could ever compare to loving a good man. No matter how important, how meaningful, teaching was, it couldn't fulfill her needs as a woman. She had never felt lonelier in her life. How different would her life be at the center of a family that shared their laughter and their tears, and fought like bears to protect one another? The thought of being a mother to Brandy and Cowboy was as appealing to her as the thought of cuddling up with their father and making passionate love to him before drifting off to sleep each night for the rest of her life. How she longed to fill that big, rambling ranch with a brood of little brothers and sisters for Cowboy and Brandy. Just thinking about sharing Judson's bed and his life in every way made her shiver.

Carrie pulled the covers up to her chin and studied the same black spot on the ceiling that held her so entranced.

Enough was enough, she told herself for what she promised was truly the last time. What was the use in fantasizing about things that were never to be? The bottom line was that she could not force her love on a family that wouldn't accept it.

Lying in the dark, Carrie wrestled with a course of action. Should she simply run home to Mom and Dad and admit they were right? Turn in her resignation at the end of the term, go back to school and start an entirely different career—one in which she wouldn't have to offer her heart up on a platter every day to those students who demanded nothing less from her? Could she possibly continue in her present position and pretend there was absolutely nothing but a professional relationship between Judson and her?

She couldn't imagine treating Judson with nothing but polite courtesy at all those school functions he was guaranteed to attend. She was not an actress. And Judson was not just another school district patron.

He was the man she loved.

Hopelessly. Passionately. Madly.

How long she lay in the dark listening to the chronic ills of her trailer, she didn't know. Squeezing her eyes shut, she tried to block the stirring images that replayed in her mind. Images of haunted blue eyes and a scarred back too wide to encircle in the span of her open arms.

Carrie punched a pillow wet from her tears.

A loud pounding on her front door brought her to her feet. Telling herself it was simply the beating of her heart against the wind's relentless serenade, Carrie stumbled from the bed and made her way to the front door. She put an eye up to the peephole and peered into the night.

The wounded wind clawed at the figure leaning on her porch. Carrie blinked hard. Twice.

It couldn't be Judson. He was in bed, resting.

Disgruntled at being awakened at such an ungodly hour, Mother waddled out of her pen on the porch. Finding her nemesis to be the cause of all the commotion, she proceeded to attack his pant leg with a viciousness that underscored her opinion of the cad who had made her mistress cry.

Hopping from foot to foot, Judson refrained from kicking the silly old goose over the moon.

"Carrie, let me in!" he begged.

She tore the door open, expecting him to fall weakly into her arms. But Judson did no such thing. He shook Mother off his leg, stepped inside and quickly closed the door behind him. His presence filled her tiny living room as he did her heart—completely.

"What are you doing up?" she cried in genuine concern for his health.

There was a dangerous glitter in his eye as he took her in. Wearing nothing but an old football jersey, Carrie made his blood simmer with desire. Pale and shaky, she was the most beautiful, desirable creature he had ever seen. It wasn't easy for him to hold himself back. He wanted to ravage her, but knowing that her innocence was as precious a gift as a woman could ever give a man, Judson would not accept it without giving her total commitment in return.

"I came for you," he said simply.

His voice was hoarse and hard. He looked at Carrie as if he could never get enough of her. He was the luckiest man in the world to find a soul mate so intelligent, so beguiling, so funny, so pure. And if he let her get away, he would surely be the dumbest on the face of the earth.

"How can we—"

"We'll make it work," Judson interrupted with the conviction of a man who knew his mind and his heart.

On the trip over, he and his children had come to an understanding. They wanted Carrie as part of their family. They needed her.

From the minute Brandy had told him what she had said to drive Carrie away, Judson worried that he had lost her for good. If only he could hold her in his arms once again, he vowed to never let her go until he told her what was in his heart.

"What about the children?" Carrie asked in a strangled whisper.

"What about them? The thought of a ready-made family too overwhelming for you?"

The question brought tears to her eyes. Her love for his children was as natural as sunshine and just as obvious to anyone watching them together. Judson could have as easily asked her to stop breathing as to question her feelings toward the two urchins who had taken her heart captive.

"The problem isn't with the way I feel about your children. It's how Brandy feels about me. There's a dark curtain covering her eyes, and I'm afraid I'll never be able to tear it down."

Touched by the poetry of her words, Judson wondered if there wasn't a trace of Indian in her blood. Carrie was a healer of hearts, a medicine woman with vast powers of which she seemed totally unaware. Whatever she'd said to Brandy had had a profound effect upon her. He could sense it in the way she had talked with him and her brother on the way over here. It was as if she had taken a giant step toward maturity while he lay sleeping. Truly, Carrie was a shaman.

As amazing as it seemed, this remarkable woman loved him. And his family. He had heard Carrie say so himself. And he longed to hear her say it again. Every day for the rest of his life.

Stepping to the door, he gestured broadly in the direction of his still-running pickup. Moments later both Cowboy and Brandy were inside, filling her small living room to maximum capacity.

"We're here to propose," Cowboy said with a grin wide enough to split his face in two. "We're a package deal, you know."

Carrie's heart tripped over enough beats to alarm a cardiologist. The boy was a perfect gem. Sweet, open, unaffected and so incredibly easy to love. But surely he had spoken out of turn. Marriage might be an appealing option to Cowboy, but Carrie was certain neither his sister nor his father saw it that way.

Short of hog-tying him, I don't think there's any way to ever get him to make that trip to the altar again—and definitely not with another white gal, Estelle had warned.

Can't you see we don't need you? Brandy had shouted.

"A package deal?" Carrie repeated. "Complete with a matched set of angels?"

Her smile was strained as she tried to make light of the sweetest words she had ever heard. "Any extras included in that deal?"

"All the horses you could want!" came Cowboy's instant rejoinder.

Thinking he'd clearly cinched the deal by himself, the boy hugged Carrie so tightly he threatened to cut off her oxygen supply. As she placed a kiss squarely on the top of his thick, black hair, Judson cleared his throat behind them.

"As much as I appreciate the thought, son, a man needs to propose for himself."

Carrie steeled herself against the inevitable. *Here it comes, the big brush-off.* She took comfort in the fact that with an audience he would surely have to let her down gently. If those sexy dimples on either side of his smile were any indication, he was going to try to keep things light.

"There's something I need to say first, Daddy."

Spared by the timely interruption, Carrie looked straight into Brandy's stormy blue eyes. The girl wore a look of grave intensity.

"I didn't mean what I said to you earlier," she said in a painful rush.

"Yes, you did, and it's okay," Carrie replied softly. "You're entitled to your feelings. I know you've been hurt in the past, Brandy, and that you're afraid I'm going to steal your father away from you. But nothing could be further from the truth. No matter how unlovable you try to make yourself, what terrible stunts you may pull, or how horribly angry you get, I'm going to still love you—and your brother—and your father. I'm going to love you no matter what until all that scared old junk around your heart finally dissolves. Regardless of what happens between your father and me, I'm just going to keep right on loving you."

A strangled cry emanated from somewhere deep inside the girl as she stepped into Carrie's open arms and was welcomed into her heart.

Carrie looked at Judson through a sheen of tears.

He doubted whether he deserved this beautiful woman, but if it took the rest of his life, he intended to prove just how much he loved her in return. His voice lost its ragged edge. Its husky timbre filled the crowded room.

"I don't exactly know how everything will exactly all work out, but I just know that I love you and I want to marry you."

Did Carrie hear correctly? Was this simply the ramblings of a delirious man who had suffered a serious blow to the head? Carrie looked deeply into his eyes for any sign of hesitancy—or remorse. The lust glittering in those piercing orbs was tempered by the light of love. Their feelings for one another were as crystal-clear as the stars peeking down at them from the darkened sky. There was no need of words. Peace and contentment and joy such as she had never known before welled up inside her. Nothing in her life compared to standing in the midst of this family, basking in their love and acceptance.

If a child of twelve was brave enough to face her fears, could Carrie do any less than pluck out the misgivings Scott had planted in her heart with his cruelty and infidelity? What kind of a person would hold on to agonizing pain rather than grasp at a chance for true happiness? Only a coward.

"Say yes," Cowboy prompted in a loud whisper.

Yes, there was nothing she wanted more in this world

than to marry him. Yes, she wanted to be a part of Brandy's and Cowboy's lives. Yes, she wanted to give him more children. Yes, she wanted to be his wife in every sense of the word.

Yes, Yes, Yes!

Judson's lips claimed hers with infinite promise. He was tender as he dragged her against him and gave her a taste of his passion. With a mouth hot on hers, Carrie moaned a soft surrender as the deep ache inside her burst into an iridescent glow pulsing in every cell in her body. The need was there and would be forever.

Nothing that felt so totally right could possibly be wrong. Her heart, her mind, her soul already belonged to this man. Joining their names legally was just a natural progression of that love.

Scattering kisses upon the rugged surface of his face, she pressed her yielding softness against his hard body and trailed an erotic path down the strong cords of Judson's neck along the scars that lashed the top of his shoulders.

"I'll take that as a yes," he purred in a feral, deep tone that sent a tugging ache low in Carrie's stomach.

"Yes," she answered, sealing it with another kiss.

Tossing his hat into the air, Cowboy sent up a rodeo grandstand cheer. Brandy merely smiled the smile of a blossoming young woman learning that love takes the courage to let go. Already she felt it returning to her manifold.

Carrie was certain that everything was going to be all right. Together they had taken the first—the hardest—step toward healing the family circle. The cycle of pain was broken at last. Though the past was written in a pattern of scars, the future was embodied in the ring that Judson would soon slip on her finger.

A ring of love, of joy, and of hope.

She would marry this man, and their lives would be forever entwined. Through the good times and the bad. Drawn out of the shadow of fear into the light of love, they had slain the frightful demons of the past together. The future was spirited by love and trust.

As long as no secrets lingered between them, no obstacles could tear them apart. Like the hallowed ground of Judson's Native American ancestors, their love was a sacred place where no intruders could tread. At long last Carrie found what she been seeking all her life. It was her most cherished dream, finding a heart and making it home. *Home,* the place where mind and soul and body come together in perfect Harmony.

*   *   *   *   *

Watch for another strong, rugged hero in Cathleen's next novel, 100% PURE COWBOY, coming February 1998 from Silhouette Romance.

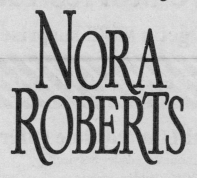

Take 4 bestselling love stories FREE

Plus get a FREE surprise gift!

Special Limited-time Offer

Mail to Silhouette Reader Service™

3010 Walden Avenue
P.O. Box 1867
Buffalo, N.Y. 14240-1867

YES! Please send me 4 free Silhouette Romance™ novels and my free surprise gift. Then send me 6 brand-new novels every month, which I will receive months before they appear in bookstores. Bill me at the low price of $2.67 each plus 25¢ delivery and applicable sales tax, if any.* That's the complete price and a savings of over 10% off the cover prices—quite a bargain! I understand that accepting the books and gift places me under no obligation ever to buy any books. I can always return a shipment and cancel at any time. Even if I never buy another book from Silhouette, the 4 free books and the surprise gift are mine to keep forever.

215 BPA A3UT

Name	(PLEASE PRINT)	
Address	Apt. No.	
City	State	Zip

This offer is limited to one order per household and not valid to present Silhouette Romance™ subscribers. *Terms and prices are subject to change without notice. Sales tax applicable in N.Y.

USROM-696　　　　　　　　　　　　　　　　©1990 Harlequin Enterprises Limited

MEN!

The good ones aren't hard to find—they're right here in Silhouette Romance!

MAN: Rick McBride, Dedicated Police Officer
MOTTO: "I always get the bad guy, but no good woman will ever get me!"

Find out how Rick gets tamed in Phyllis Halldorson's
THE LAWMAN'S LEGACY. (October 1997)

MAN: Tucker Haynes, Undercover Investigator
MOTTO: "I'll protect a lady in need until the danger ends, but I'll protect my heart forever."

Meet the woman who shatters this
gruff guy's walls in Laura Anthony's
THE STRANGER'S SURPRISE. (November 1997)

MAN: Eric Bishop, The Ultimate Lone Wolf
MOTTO: "I'm back in town to find my lost memories, *not* to make new ones."

Discover what secrets—and romance—are in store
when this loner comes home in Elizabeth August's
PATERNAL INSTINCTS. (December 1997)

We've handpicked the strongest, bravest, sexiest heroes yet! Don't miss these exciting books from

Silhouette ROMANCE™

Available at your favorite retail outlet.

Look us up on-line at: http://www.romance.net   MEN

You've been waiting for him all your life....
Now your Prince has finally arrived!

In fact, *three* handsome princes
are coming your way in

ROYAL WEDDINGS

A delightful new miniseries by **LISA KAYE LAUREL**
about three bachelor princes who find happily-ever-
after with three small-town women!

Coming in September 1997—THE PRINCE'S BRIDE

Crown Prince Erik Anders would do anything for his
country—even plan a pretend marriage to his lovely
castle caretaker. But could he convince the king, and
the rest of the world, that his proposal was real—before
his cool heart melted for his small-town "bride"?

Coming in November 1997—THE PRINCE'S BABY

Irresistible Prince Whit Anders was shocked to
discover that the summer romance he'd had years
ago had resulted in a very royal baby! Now that
pretty Drew Davis's secret was out, could her kiss
turn the sexy prince into a full-time dad?

**Look for prince number three in the exciting
conclusion to ROYAL WEDDINGS,
coming in 1998—only from**

▼*Silhouette* ROMANCE™